CARIDAD S
THE SPANISH GOLL

A Little Betrayal Among Friends

The Labyrinth of Desire

The Monster in the Garden

Translated and freely adapted

By

Caridad Svich

Santa Catalina Editions/NoPassport imprint

The Spanish Golden Age Plays by Caridad Svich

Santa Catalina Editions/NoPassport imprint;
www.nopassport.org

ISBN: 978-1-300-17672-5

The Spanish Golden Age Plays

A LITTLE BETRAYAL AMONG FRIENDS

THE LABYRINTH OF DESIRE

THE MONSTER IN THE GARDEN

The three plays in his collection are all translations and free adaptations of comedies from the Spanish Golden Age by authors Maria Zayas de Sotomayor, Lope de Vega, and Calderon de la Barca. Although they were commissioned by different theatre organizations, they constitute, for me, a trilogy of romantic comedies that examine gender, sexuality, Identity, from disparate yet related points of view The comedies all delight in the play with formal theatrical conventions, and are distinguished by a piquant wit, energy and mystery. In the end, they all offer profound and unique meditations on love and the ends to which we humans will go to achieve and sustain it.

A little betrayal among friends

By

Caridad Svich

freely adapted/translated
from Maria de Zayas y Sotomayor's
La Traicion en la amistad
(approx. 1628-1632)

Script History:

This adaptation was originally commissioned in 2006 by Airmid Theatre, New York, (Tricia McDermott, Artistic Director), with support from Open Meadows Foundation and New York State Council of the Arts. This play received its premiere as part of the Airmid Theatre Summer Festival at Nissequogue River State Park in Kings Park, NY in July 2011 under Tricia McDermott's direction.

María de Zayas y Sotomayor
By Jennifer Adams

María de Zayas y Sotomayor (September 12, 1590–1661) wrote during Spain's Golden Age of literature. She is considered by a number of modern critics as one of the pioneers of modern literary feminism, while others consider her simply a well-accomplished baroque author. The female characters in de Zayas' stories were used as vehicles to enlighten readers about the plight of women in Spanish society, or to instruct them in proper ways to live their lives. Born in Madrid, de Zayas was the daughter of infantry captain Fernando de Zayas y Sotomayor and María Catalina de Barrasa. So very little is known about her life that it is not even certain whether she was single or married during the time she wrote. What is known is that she was fortunate to belong to the aristocracy of Madrid, because despite earning the low salary typical of writers at the time, she lived well. In 1637, de Zayas published her first collection of novellas, *Novelas Amorosas y Ejemplares (The Enchantments of Love)* in Zaragoza, and ten years later, her second collection, *Desengaños Amorosos (The Disenchantments of Love)*, was published. De Zayas also composed a play, *La traicion en la Amistad, (Friendship Betrayed)* as well as several poems. The author enjoyed the respect and admiration of some of the best male writers of her day. Among her many admirers were Lope de Vega, who dedicated some of his poetry to her, and Alonso de Castillo Solórzano, who named her the "Sibila de Madrid," (Sibyl of Madrid). Despite the enduring popularity of her works during the seventeenth and eighteenth centuries, the nineteenth-century saw her works censured for their perceived vulgarity. As a result, they faded into obscurity, and would remain obscure until the late twentieth century. The exact day of her death remains a mystery. Death certificates bearing the name María de Zayas have been found in both 1661 and 1669, yet neither seems to belong to her. De Zayas' most successful works are her *Novelas Amorosas y ejemplares (Amorous and Exemplary Novels)*, published in 1637, and *Desengaños Amorosos (Disenchantments of Love)*, published in 1647. They are known as the Spanish Decameron because they followed a structure used by the Italian writer Giovanni Bocaccio, which consisted of many framed novelle within one. These novellas, which were written in a complex style, were a very popular genre in all of Europe. De Zayas was strongly influenced by Miguel de Cervantes' *"Novelas ejemplares (Exemplary Novels)* which were also written in the style of the Italian novellà. Use of the genre allowed de Zayas the flexibility to share many stories and while developing several strong characters, and provided a great showcase for her range.

The two works feature the central character, Lisis, who has invited a group of her friends to her home to help her recover from an illness. In an attempt to lift her spirits, each of her friends narrates a story about a particular experience. Two stories are narrated per night for a total of five nights. While the first book describes violence and deception, the second one intensifies these themes. The second book is full of description which displays, without censure, the abuse of women. The female characters in both books are well developed, and their experience allows them to eloquently denounce their inferior role in society: *Why vain legislators of the world, do you tie our hands so that we cannot take vengeance? Because of your mistaken ideas about us, you render us powerless and deny us access to pen and sword. Isn't our soul the same as a man's soul?.... [Later the husband listens her laments and approaches Laura] moving closer to her and incesed in an infernal rage, (Diego) began to beat her with his hands, so much so that the white pearls of her teeth, bathed in the blood shed by his angry hand, quickly took on the form of red coral (tran. H. Patoy Boyor, The Enchantments of Love)*

As recently as the early 1980s, scant attention was devoted to female writers of the Golden Age of Spain. Within a decade, this changed dramatically, as scholars began to turn their attention to close studies of the women writers of this era. Interest in "Gynocriticism," the study of women writers, grew considerably during the 1990s, and much of the interest focusing on de Zayas' work, which depicted women as strong and intelligent individuals. Many of de Zayas' characters have been wronged by men, and they have embarked on a journey to regain their honour. Emilia Pardo Bazán helped to bring Zayas' work once again to the forefront. Bazan described Zayas' stories of the aristocracy of Madrid.

In *The Cultural Labyrinth of Maria de Zayas*, Marina Brownlee argues that de Zayas' novellas were greatly influenced by Baroque culture, and were represented by a series of paradoxes. Brownlee explains how de Zayas' women were themselves a paradox: the women were strong of character, but not strong enough to escape their particular negative situations. According to Brownlee, de Zayas' belief was that the source of violence was the family, which was in turn an extension of a bigger institution, the Inquisition. She also points out that de Zayas' women were atypical females who chose to fight for revenge and defy their roles toward gender, race, sexuality, and class.

Echoing Brownlee's commentaries, Lisa Vollendorf's *Reclaiming the Body: Maria de Zayas' Early Modern Feminism* argues that de Zayas used her prose to challenge the social view toward women. Vollendorf claims that de Zayas' use of vivid images were intended for this purpose. She also explores de Zayas' strong belief in the convent as a haven for women's independence. According to Vollendorf, de Zayas had little expectation for change to occur by itself, and she became a voice urging women to seek independence and men to educate themselves about violence.

De Zayas distinguished herself by writing about violence against women within the context of a "gender system" in Spain which was too universally accepted to change. She wrote within the confines of the Spanish Inquisition, during a time when women were closely monitored and kept from participating in any significant decision-making in the society. The paternalistic society of 17th century Spain dictated the confinement of the majority of the women to the home, the convent, or brothels, and it was fortunate for de Zayas that she was born into privilege and was able to avoid living this type of existence.

De Zayas' *Desengaños amorosos* became a literary milestone by presenting women as intelligent people who could present and defend arguments in the style of an "academia." The women are independent and show they don't need a male to discourse on intelligent topics, and they are more than capable of following the same practical ground rules and protocols as the men do. The general theme of the arguments is the mistreatment of women at the hands of men. This desire for female camaraderie and independence was contrary to most of the portrayals of women of the era, and was a unique way of portraying women in a world where the men of the society were looked to for guidance and leadership. During the 20th century, the feminist literary canon in Spain was limited to one or two female writers. But de Zayas and other writers of the seventeenth century, including her fellow Spaniard Ana Caro and

England's Aphra Behn, have been rediscovered by academics seeking to uncover or re-discover other first-rate works by unconventional voices.

Given the vision and excellence of her work, the public's desire to know more about the mysterious life of de Zayas is understandable. But it is this very lack of knowledge about her personal life which may prove advantageous to her legacy, because it places the reader's attention solely on her work.

Introduction: Love's Treason

By Caridad Svich

Approximately three hundred and seventy years before *Sex and the City* and *Gossip Girl*, there was Maria Zayas de Sotomayor's *La traicion en la amistad*. An esteemed, popular novelist during the Spanish Golden Age, Zayas also wrote poems, essays and several plays before withdrawing from a life in letters. *La traicion...*(likely completed in 1632) however is her only extant play. As such, it offers a rare theatrical glimpse into the life of upper-class women in the 17th century. While Zayas follows the conventions that friendly colleague Lope de Vega and others of the period made to the *comedia* and its form - compact, swift, and bound by themes of love and honor - Zayas differs in *La traicion...* by revolving her plot around circuitous patterns of behavior rather than elements of chance, destiny and design. She keeps establishing conventional modes of action and then subverting them for other concerns, chief of which is the exposure and ridicule of her male lead Lysander – a slippery-tongued, late-blooming misogynist, and her female anti-heroine Felicia – a sexually free playgirl. Zayas has mixed feelings for all her characters, if not a dose of compassion. Clearly she wants to empower Felicia and unbind her from the standards of honor and virtue, but at the same time, she is conflicted by Felicia's lack of moral conscience, especially in regard to her friendships with other women. The play circles around comic sequences that center on the expectation of love (amorous and platonic) and its betrayal, whether overt or indirect. Zayas, therefore, is contemplating how betrayal is possibly an inevitable part of opening your heart to another, be it friend, lover or stranger. It is not a sweet sentiment, and indeed, the upper-class circle that Zayas depicts is cousin to the one depicted in Choderlos De Laclos' *Les Liasons Dangereuses* (1782). Yet, unlike De Laclos, Zayas has faith in her characters' renewal. They are not fixed from the outset, but rather, capable of change or at very least, awareness of their actions. There is research to indicate that Zayas, in writing this play, was responding directly to Tirso de Molina's *Don Juan/lel burlador de sevilla.* It is tantalizing to read Zayas' play as an inversion of Tirso's classic, but I think Zayas was after something more in this play than simply one-upping Tirso. Zayas is seeking to unravel the knot of love itself and how it enters lives; she wants to examine the glory and simultaneous wreckage of love. In the two previous English-language faithful, scholarly translations of this play (by Teresa S. Soufas, 1997; and Catherine Larson with notes by Valerie Hegstrom, 1999), every effort has been made to read Zayas' work through a feminist lens.

As free interpreter, adaptor and translator of this text, I have been faced with the dilemma of re-recording Zayas's vision for a new age, but also making the play work on the stage. The solution of preferring prose

14

over strict meter and rhyme scheme is not the only one toward addressing the play's inherent unconventionality and movable anchors. Unlike male writers of this period in dramatic history, Zayas' work in relatively unknown to theatre-goers and practitioners (though recognized by academics and scholars). So, in many ways, working on and staging this play, is very much like staging a brand new play. Its precedents are unfamiliar, its situations, however, are not. You don't need to know Spanish Golden Age drama to appreciate Zayas' comedy, and I also think that reducing her point of view to a feminist one (as valid as it is) negates the problematics of the piece itself, which is conflicted and somewhat at war with not only the position of women in society but also how women and men behave toward themselves and each other.

Love's treason – its blessed and cursed treachery on our inviolate hearts – is the focus of this play. In this free adaptation (working from my own translation), I have cut entire scenes and characters from the original, changed motivations and intentions, and added new text – all, though, in order to meet what I believe are Zayas' original purposes. Any free version will bear the mark of its author. And this case is no different. Zayas is interested in the machinations and inconsistencies of love and its pursuit (and she reflects this both in content and form). My own interests as a playwright are attracted to the unexplained, irrational forces that govern passion and how those forces can disrupt relationships and the form of theatre itself. *A little betrayal among friends,* thus, is my answer to Zayas. Love's enchanting *traicion* destabilizes the vision that we carry of ourselves and instead offers us the un-fixed possibilities of who we can be. It is in the spirit of possibility that I offer this text.

Figures:

MARCIA, sweet-natured young, upper-class woman with a feisty streak

FELICIA*, free-spirited, mischievous young upper-class woman

DON JUAN, legendary bachelor and playboy

LYSANDER*, the object of everyone's affection, handsome young man, a cad

LEON, his assistant, honest, if a bit blunt

GERRY*, Marcia's former lover, good-hearted, shy; also plays FELIX, Laura's loyal confidante.

LAURA, Lysander's former lover, impetuous and naturally high-strung

The Setting: The present. A cosmopolitan city full of secret alleys and unsuspecting mazes.

Notes: *In the source text, Felicia is originally named Fenisa, Lysander is originally named Liseo, and Gerry is originally named Gerardo. Melody to the original song by Caridad Svich in the text may be obtained by contacting the author, or her lyrics may be re-set by another composer.

ACT ONE, Scene 1

[Marcia and Felicia enter.]

MARCIA: I'm in love.
FELICIA: Are you sure?
MARCIA: Of course I'm sure. Lysander's the only man for me. I knew it from the moment he laid eyes on me.
FELICIA: That must have been quite a look he gave you.
MARCIA: His eyes went straight through me. It was as if he could read not only every part of my body, save my very soul.
FELICIA: And so, you yielded to love.
MARCIA: I had no choice.
FELICIA: You always have a choice.
MARCIA: Not when it comes to love.
FELICIA: Marcia, you're fooling yourself.
MARCIA: I want Lysander. Is that a crime?
FELICIA: No, but –
MARCIA: I can't be like you, Felicia.
FELICIA: What does that mean? I've been in love.
MARCIA: Yes, of course, Felicia, you've been in love.
FELICIA: If I don't always give in to it…
MARCIA: I'm not giving in.
FELICIA: You're swearing yourself to Lysander. Just like that.
MARCIA: Well, wouldn't you?
[Marcia shows Felicia a photo of Lysander]
FELICIA: Is this him?

MARCIA: Say it. He's delicious.

FELICIA: *(aside)* He's more than that. If I don't have him, I'll die.

MARCIA: What's that?

FELICIA: He's handsome, no question. But there are many handsome men.

MARCIA: There are many fish in the sea, but we don't all eat them, is that what you mean?

FELICIA: I don't mean anything. I mean… well, what about Gerry?

MARCIA: What about him?

FELICIA: He adores you. He's adored you for quite some time now.

MARCIA: Let him adore me. I'll adore Lysander.

FELICIA: You'll forget Lysander soon enough.

MARCIA: What makes you say that?

FELICIA: You forgot Gerry as soon as you saw Lysander, didn't you?

MARCIA: I'm not fickle.

FELICIA: No, but it's better to love someone who already loves you than to put your blind faith in someone you only want to love.

MARCIA: I love Lysander through and through. This isn't simply about desire.

FELICIA: There's nothing simple about desire.

MARCIA: You think I can't love, is that it?

FELICIA: I didn't say that.

MARCIA: Just because you go around…

FELICIA: What?

MARCIA: Doing things.

FELICIA: What kind of things?

MARCIA: You know what I mean.

FELICIA: I'm afraid I don't.

MARCIA: No one can keep up with you. Who's Felicia with this week?

FELICIA: And who isn't she with.

MARCIA: I don't know how you can do it.

FELICIA: I'm an animal.

MARCIA: Don't say that.

FELICIA: I am. We all are. Why shouldn't we give in to our instincts?

MARCIA: Because we're not mere animals.

FELICIA: No, but if I see a man I want....Well, I just have to have him.

MARCIA: And have your heart broken in the process.

FELICIA: That's where you're mistaken. My heart's unbreakable.

MARCIA: Really?

FELICIA: I go in full of base love. I go out full of base love. My heart is as solid as a stone.

MARCIA: Except when it comes to Don Juan.

FELICIA: You had to bring him up, didn't you? You couldn't leave well enough alone.

MARCIA: You still love him, don't you?

FELICIA: I never loved him.

MARCIA: Is that so?

FELICIA: He's the one who loves me. He's like your Gerry. Don Juan's besotted. Poor thing.

MARCIA: He is not.

FELICIA: He will be. By the time I'm through with him

MARCIA: The things you say…

FELICIA: Well, what should I say?

MARCIA: You could leave Don Juan alone.

FELICIA: Out of pity? .

MARCIA: Well….why not?

FELICIA: …I can't.
I won't. After all he's done…
No. Tit for effing tat.
He plays hard, I'll play harder.
He wants me? He loves me?
I'll make him work for it.
It's a game, you see?
It's not that I want him.
Don Juan? He's not my type.
But he's come after me, right?
And to what end?
Just so that I can be another conquest?
No. I won't be another name in his little book.
My love is worth more than that.

MARCIA: So, you don't love him?

FELICIA: What would I do with Don Juan?
Don Juan can go to hell
(as the writers and philosophers have proclaimed for
centuries)
But before he does, let him have a good taste of me,
Of Felicia, of glorious Felicia,
And I am glorious and wondrous
and everything a woman should and can be!

MARCIA: Spoken modestly.

FELICIA: I know what I'm worth. And so should he.
Let him crave me mind and body - he can go to his
grave forever missing me.

MARCIA: You're cruel.

FELICIA: And you've a lot of feeling all of sudden for good ol' Don Juan. Why's that? You prefer him now to Gerry and Lysander?

MARCIA: No. I just think

FELICIA: What?

MARCIA: One should go into love, any kind of love, with…clarity.

FELICIA: Like you with Lysander?

MARCIA: Exactly.

FELICIA: Deliver us, O Lord, from such clarity.

MARCIA: Why is my love for Lysander so hard for you to understand?

FELICIA: It's not for me to question.

MARCIA: No. It's not. Not one bit. Or is it….?

FELICIA: What?

MARCIA: Nothing.

FELICIA: Marcia, if you've something to say to me, say it.

MARCIA: All right, but I want you to be honest with me.

FELICIA: Of course.

MARCIA: Swear.

FELICIA: What is this?

MARCIA: Swear.

FELICIA: Okay. I swear. What is it?

MARCIA: …Do you want Lysander for yourself?

FELICIA: What?

MARCIA: You heard me.

FELICIA: I can't believe…

MARCIA: Do you?

FELICIA: I wouldn't dream of it.
MARCIA: You're lying.
FELICIA: Marcia, I'm your friend.
MARCIA: If you were my friend, you'd want me to be happy.
FELICIA: And I do. I want nothing more. I just don't want to see you get hurt, that's all.
MARCIA: And why would I get hurt, unless you plan on taking him away from me?
FELICIA: How can you say such a thing?
MARCIA: Because I know you. You're insatiable.
FELICIA: I love freely. Is that a crime?
MARCIA: Only when it interferes with your friend's happiness.
FELICIA: Marcia, I only want what's best for you.
MARCIA: Felicia, how do you know what's best for me? You can't read my heart.
FELICIA: You're in love. I'm outside it. I can see things more clearly.
MARCIA: Please.
FELICIA: Marcia…
MARCIA: Not one more word. If you can't speak well of Lysander, then don't speak to me at all.

[Marcia exits]

FELICIA: Love has caught her. That's for sure.
But as it catches her,
it too infects me with its sweet poison.
I'll see Lysander. And I'll make him mine.
Not because I'm not a good friend, but because

I'm also ruled by love's mad design.
Where love rules, friendship falls by the wayside
(It's unfortunate, but true).
My soul's on fire. And Cupid's blind.

Scene 2

[Don Juan appears]

DON JUAN: I knew I'd find you.
FELICIA: I didn't know you were looking for me.
DON JUAN: How could I not look for beautiful
Felicia, light of my soul…
FELICIA: You flatter me, Don Juan.
DON JUAN: What if I do? Grant me your favor
awhile. I'm in a bad way.
FELICIA: What now?
DON JUAN: I'm in love, and you're ignoring me.
FELICIA: *(aside)* Why shouldn't I ignore him when I
have Lysander in mind? In truth, there's room in my
heart for a million lovers.
DON JUAN: You're cruel, unforgiving…
FELICIA: And you're jealous.
DON JUAN: Jealousy's a soft word. What I am: is
dead…you hear me? Dead if you don't care for me.
FELICIA: Has it come to that? I thought you were
made of stronger stuff, Don Juan.
DON JUAN: You mock me.
FELICIA: I do nothing of the kind. I care for you very
much. I'm…distracted. That's all.
DON JUAN: What's driving you to distraction?

FELICIA: Talk.

DON JUAN: What kind of talk?

FELICIA: Talk of a young man.

DON JUAN: A young man?

FELICIA: A handsome young man every woman in our circle seems to be falling for…Do you know who I mean?

DON JUAN: Well, I…

FELICIA: Starts with an L.

DON JUAN: An L?

FELICIA: Can you guess?

DON JUAN: Lysander?

FELICIA: I'm so glad you're on top of things.

DON JUAN: If only I were….Look, if you think I'm going to tell you anything about him…

FELICIA: I wouldn't dream of it. You're Don Juan, after all. What's a Lysander to you? Just another man.

DON JUAN: You're in love with him, aren't you?

FELICIA: Why do you say that?

DON JUAN: It's written all over you.

FELICIA: I'm not that transparent.

DON JUAN: You are to me.

FELICIA: You think you've got me, don't you?

DON JUAN: I know you.

FELICIA: You don't know the half of me.

DON JUAN: Teach me, then.

FELICIA: I won't be your instructor.

DON JUAN: You don't like that game?

FELICIA: It doesn't suit me.

DON JUAN: Would you rather I taught you, then?

FELICIA: What could you teach me?

DON JUAN: How to love….properly.

FELICIA: Is my love improper?

DON JUAN: It's cold.

FELICIA: I thought that's how you liked it. Cold and fast.

DON JUAN: I like feeling.

FELICIA: Inflicting feeling or giving feeling?

DON JUAN: Don't toy with me, Felicia.

FELICIA: Don't order me, Don Juan.

DON JUAN: You confuse a request with an order. I wonder how you were brought up.

FELICIA: Same as you.

DON JUAN: Not the same.

FELICIA: Same class.

DON JUAN: Different sex.

FELICIA: What difference does that make?

DON JUAN: All the difference in the world.

FELICIA: And if I told you I was raised as a man?

DON JUAN: I wouldn't believe you.

FELICIA: Why not?

DON JUAN: Look at you.

FELICIA: What do my looks have to do with my sex?

DON JUAN: Everything.

FELICIA: I could love you as a man.

DON JUAN: But I wouldn't love you in kind.

FELICIA: Would it upset your equilibrium?

DON JUAN: Not in the least, but there is the matter of desire…

FELICIA: Fickle desire.

DON JUAN: Honest desire.

FELICIA: I didn't know desire had the property of honesty.

DON JUAN: It's the only property it possesses completely.

FELICIA: Since when?

DON JUAN: Time immemorial.

FELICIA: Does your memory go back that far?

DON JUAN: Enough now, Felicia.

FELICIA: You've had enough of me? Well then, go your way, Don Juan. Let's end this charade.

DON JUAN: Stop.

FELICIA: How are you going to stop me?

DON JUAN: …I'll hold you.

FELICIA: And then?

DON JUAN: And then we'll see.

FELICIA: …You'll tire of me.

DON JUAN: I'll never tire of you. You're my love; I've never been surer of anything than I am of this: You are my star among stars, my heart's intoxicating elixir, radiant beam of…

FELICIA: Let go of me.

DON JUAN: Felicia…

FELICIA: Let go.

DON JUAN: I'll hurt you.

FELICIA: You wouldn't dare.

DON JUAN: Don't push me.

FELICIA: But you like being pushed, and shoved, and put into a corner, little boy.

DON JUAN: Yes. I do, ma'am. Sometimes. And sometimes I'd rather be free. But you won't let me.

FELICIA: I've no hold on you.

DON JUAN: Oh, but you do. You've seen to it. Haven't you?

FELICIA: What are you talking about?

DON JUAN: You've bewitched me.

FELICIA: You're like out of some book.

DON JUAN: I'm Don Juan. What do you expect?

FELICIA: I expect you'd want to be free of your story.

DON JUAN: We're born with one story, we die with one story.

FELICIA: Stories can change.

DON JUAN: Like love.

FELICIA: Your love changes.

DON JUAN: If my love was once changeable, it's not anymore. You've seen to it, Felicia. You've made sure that I'd go around…following you everywhere like your dog.

FELICIA: Bark all you like.

DON JUAN: Have a little heart.

FELICIA: You sound like a song.

DON JUAN: Stay with me. Please.

FELICIA: …That line may work with other women, but not me.

DON JUAN: Stay.

FELICIA: Why should I?

DON JUAN: Isn't my love enough?

FELICIA: No. It's not.

DON JUAN: Felicia!

FELICIA: …If you're going to hurt me, hurt me now. Get it over with. I'll scratch your eyes out until there isn't any blood left.

DON JUAN: I wouldn't hurt you. I'd never…

FELICIA: You love me too much?

DON JUAN: Yes.

FELICIA: Good.

DON JUAN: Revenge doesn't become you, dear.

FELICIA: Does it make me hard?

DON JUAN: As a matter of fact, it does.

FELICIA: Pity you can only love soft women, pliant women….

DON JUAN: I've loved all kinds. You know that. But respect… there's always been that between us.

FELICIA: I'm sorry, am I not respecting you? Oh, I'm so sorry, sir. But I seem to recall you went off with what's-her-name and what's-her-other-name the same night we made love.

DON JUAN: You know me. As I know you. You'd do the same.

FELICIA: That's where you're wrong.

That's the lesson you haven't learned about me.

I love. Yes. All sorts. Yes. In that, we're the same.

But I see each love through to the end before taking another.

I don't mess about with constancy.

When I have love, I revere it.

I don't squander it like you do.

DON JUAN: You're going to begrudge me one night?

FELICIA: One night and more if I have to.

DON JUAN: And this L, this Lysander, you think he'll be different?

FELICIA: I haven't given him much thought, actually.

DON JUAN: You're not in love with him, then?

FELICIA: I only brought him up because Marcia
wants to marry him.
And as a good friend, a concerned friend,
(which is what I am, at day's end –
Regardless of what people may think or say)
I want to make sure he's the right man for her.
So, from what you can tell, from what you've seen or
heard, is he?
DON JUAN: Lysander?
FELICIA: Yes.
DON JUAN: I couldn't say.
FELICIA: Couldn't say or won't say?
DON JUAN: He's nothing to me.
FELICIA: Only a magnet for your jealousy.
DON JUAN: I'm not -
FELICIA: Don't lie to me. I know you.
Here I am filled with love for you
and I am, can't you see?
(Stupid boy. Stupid man. Crazy mad heart.)
and what do you do?
You behave like a jealous little bitch.
Well, if that's you want, that's what you'll get.
DON JUAN: What?
FELICIA: I will fall in love with Lysander.
DON JUAN: Felicia.
FELICIA : From this moment on, he'll be mine. I'll
make sure of it.
DON JUAN: Hold on now.
FELICIA: Hold nothing. I'll be his. And that's all there
is to it.

[She exits.]

DON JUAN: Felicia!

[He goes after her.]

Scene 3

[Lysander enters with Leon, his assistant.]

LEON: Look at you: happy as can be.
LYSANDER: Hmm?
LEON: Ever since Marcia declared her love for you, you've been on a cloud.
LYSANDER: Me?
LEON: Floating.
LYSANDER: So? Why shouldn't I be happy? Marcia's an angel. I've every right to bask in my good fortune.
LEON: She has that.
LYSANDER: What are you saying? That I'm only after her for her money?
LEON: Of course not.
LYSANDER: I wouldn't do that. I'm not that kind of man, Leon. I can't believe you'd think that of me.
LEON: But she does have money. Doesn't she?
LYSANDER: Yes.
LEON: So, why not be thankful? You've scored, my friend. Right on the mark. Hit the bulls-eye.
LYSANDER: What's wrong with you, Leon?
LEON: Nothing. Nothing at all.
LYSANDER: It's as if you resented that I was in love.

LEON: Oh, so, you are in love, then?

LYSANDER: Of course. Marcia's very dear to me.

LEON: Well then, that's that.

LYSANDER: That's what?

LEON: End of story.

LYSANDER: What story?

LEON: This story. You know, the one we're telling, the one we're in. This play called *A little betrayal among friends*.

LYSANDER: I don' know what you could possibly be talking about. It is definitely not the end of the story. Leon, it hasn't even started.

LEON: For you, maybe, but for me…

LYSANDER: I thought you'd be happy.

LEON: Oh, I am. I radiate happiness. Can't you see?

LYSANDER: Not really.

LEON: Best pay me more, then.

LYSANDER: I pay you plenty. You're a good assistant.

LEON: I'm baggage.

LYSANDER: You're not.

LEON: Not even part of a proper entourage.

LYSANDER: I hate entourages. They're such a waste. All those people hanging around…And for what? No. I've always been a one-assistant kind of guy.

LEON: Yes, you have. But now…You won't need me.

LYSANDER: What are you talking about?

LEON: Well, you're getting married, aren't you?

LYSANDER: Most likely.

LEON: Then it's the end.

LYSANDER: Is that what you think?

LEON: Well, look at you.

LYSANDER: What's wrong with how I look?

LEON: Nothing. But you're, well…I shouldn't say it.

LYSANDER: Go on.

LEON: No.

LYSANDER: I hate it when you do that.

LEON: Do what?

LYSANDER: Just say it, man. Spit it out.

LEON: Well, if you insist… love's made you stupid.

LYSANDER: Huh?

LEON: There's not a thought in your head except Marcia this and Marcia that, and oh Marcia…That's no way to live. No way at all. Believe me, you're better off with any one of those girls from across town any day.

LYSANDER: Cheap girls, you mean?

LEON: Absolutely. Give it up for cheap girls. They're the best.

LYSANDER: In what way?

LEON: In many ways, but if I had to pick one…

LYSANDER: Pick.

LEON: Cheap girls give, but don't fill up your head, if you know what I mean.

LYSANDER: You know, Leon, you've always been crude.

LEON: Just speaking truth.

LYSANDER: Yes, well…we've all had our fun with those girls

LEON: That we have. Good times.

LYSANDER: Wasted days.

LEON: Drunken nights. Remember that time…?

LYSANDER: In the bungalow?

LEON: Oh. God. That was…

LYSANDER: Quite a time.

LEON: Do you still have their - ?

LYSANDER: Number? No. Last I heard they left the country.

LEON: Cheap, foreign girls. That's what I'm talking about.

LYSANDER: You're a racist, sexist prick, Leon.

LEON: Whose words are those? Her words?

LYSANDER: All mine.

LEON: At least I call it how I see it, dude. No p.c. crap for me.

LYSANDER: You could use a bit of it.

LEON: Why?

LYSANDER: To rise up in the world.

LEON: Me and the rest of the hypocrites, eh? I'll keep that in mind.

LYSANDER: Look, I know what you mean: those girls, they're all right. Good time, good fun, sure, but, in the end, you can't be serious with those girls.

LEON: And why not?

LYSANDER: You just can't.

LEON: In order to rise up in the world?

LYSANDER: Yes.

LEON: Now, who's the prick?

LYSANDER: What?

LEON: Why would you want to be serious? Why complicate things? It's just sex.

LYSANDER: Leon….

LEON: Let's be frank about it: that's all you're interested in.
LYSANDER: That's all you're interested in.
LEON: And I'm right. Get your fill and move on, that's all there is to it.
LYSANDER: What about -?
LEON: Flowers? Cards?
LYSANDER: A life.
LEON: What kind of life? My mom and dad, they had a life. And what'd it get them?
LYSANDER: Death and taxes.
LEON: Absolutely. Screwed-up death, screwed-up taxes, and screwed-up fucking love. That's no way to live. I learnt my lesson. You should learn yours. Even if you've got the world and all the women in it at your feet… love's a waste. You hear me?
LYSANDER: Yes, Leon.
LEON: But these girls…
LYSANDER: The cheap ones?
LEON: Call them what you will. These girls leave you be. And if they don't, well, all you have to do is give them a good slap, and they go on their way.
LYSANDER: I can't believe you. You've no feelings at all.
LEON: What use have I for feelings? I can't afford them. If I had a bit of money in the bank, then I could afford a bit more feeling, but such as it is…
LYSANDER: I pay you plenty, Leon.
LEON: Not enough.
LYSANDER: Enough to get by.

LEON: …And if I were a girl? What would you pay me?

LYSANDER: Are you drunk?

LEON: Sober is as sober does.

LYSANDER: I think you're very drunk. On what? I don't know. But on something, that's for sure.

LEON: I'm just trying to reason with you.

LYSANDER: Well, I don't want to hear it. Understand? I don't want to hear your crap. I love Marcia. Can you get that through your head? I love her. She's the only woman for me.

LEON: Well, you better show her, then.

LYSANDER: In time, Leon.

LEON: She wants you now, man. Why are you waiting for?

LYSANDER: …Is that her?

LEON: What?

LYSANDER: Over there. On the terrace

LEON: No, that's her friend Felicia.

LYSANDER: I don't think I've met her.

LEON: She's been around.

LYSANDER: Was she at the -?

LEON: Yeah.

LYSANDER: Must've missed her somehow.

[Felicia is on the terrace.]

FELICIA: Hello, gentlemen.

LEON & LYSANDER: Hey.

FELICIA: Lucky's the woman who's favored by your love.

LYSANDER: Lucky are you for being favored by Marcia's friendship.

FELICIA: *(aside)* Hardly favored.

She's got it into her head that I'm after her Lysander.

Well, I am, but not in the way she thinks.

I mean, I love him. But I love many men.

You see, love's a divine potion. I bless myself with it.

LYSANDER: Felicia, is there any sweet word from Marcia for me?

FELICIA: Marcia? Oh. Yes. A letter.

LYSANDER: Really? That's old-fashioned.

FELICIA: I thought you liked that about her.

LYSANDER: I do. But well, I guess I just didn't expect…

FELICIA: Shall I tear it up, then?

LYSANDER: No!

FELICIA: Don't worry. I wouldn't. I'm not like that.

LEON: What are you like?

FELICIA: I'm a good friend.

LYSANDER: And what does she say in the letter?

FELICIA: Read it for yourself. You'll see.

[She tosses letter his way.] So long, gentlemen.

LEON: You're leaving already?

FELICIA: I can't stay. Sorry.

[She withdraws.]

LEON: She's a looker, eh?

LYSANDER: She's fine enough.

LEON: Likes you.

LYSANDER: How do you know?

LEON: I could tell.

LYSANDER: I'm not looking, Leon.

LEON: I know; just making an observation…

LYSANDER: My heart's set on Marcia.

LEON: As long as it's set.

LYSANDER: Firmly.

LEON: …To the letter, then…

LYSANDER: This isn't Marcia's handwriting.

LEON: Whose is it?

LYSANDER: I don't know. Do you recognize it?

LEON: Can't say that I do.

LYSANDER: A mystery.

LEON: And what does this mystery lady say?

LYSANDER: Let's see…"Brave Lysander"

LEON: That's a good start.

LYSANDER: It is, isn't it?

LEON: I don't know of any man who wouldn't want to be called brave. Go on.

LYSANDER: "Love has given me its poison and with it I write."

LEON: I don't like the sound of that.

LYSANDER: What'd you mean?

LEON: Poison.

LYSANDER: It's a metaphor.

LEON: Precisely. I hate metaphors. If you can't trust words to say what they mean, then don't say anything. That's my motto.

LYSANDER: May I go on?

LEON: Sorry. Yes.

LYSANDER: "Although somebody else loves you, I'll dare to love you. I'll risk everything, even death, for I feel as if you've already killed me with your eyes."

LEON: Intense.

LYSANDER: Seems it. "Punish me with desire."
LEON: Sweet and rough. I'd like to meet this woman.
LYSANDER: "I don't mind. I'll take your tender
punishment as it comes." At least she's honest.
LEON: More than that. She's laying it on the line,
man.
LYSANDER: "I live on St. James Street.
I'll wait for you. Behind the blue gate. At midnight.
Where you live, I live.
Where you don't, I die."
LEON: …That's quite a letter.
LYSANDER: I've never seen the like.
LEON: So, you're going to St. James Street?
LYSANDER: I need to think…
LEON: What's to think about? She's offering herself
to you. She's a sure thing. Go on. Take advantage of
it. What have you to lose?
LYSANDER: Only my heart…
LEON: What heart? Are you in some other play now?
Are you Romeo all of a sudden?
LYSANDER: Not exactly.
LEON: Then…forget your heart. It's what I've been
trying to tell you. Follow desire wherever it leads.
Look, you've got one woman who adores you, right?
LYSANDER: Marcia.
LEON: Exactly. And you've another one here who'll
literally die for you. Well, I say take what you can get,
as much as you can get.
LYSANDER: Leon…
LEON: I speak your truth, man. And you don't have
to take credit for it. You can just say "Oh, Leon, he's

the rude one, not me." But I know you through and through. You can't hide from me.

LYSANDER: Don't be so sure.

LEON: I know what you're thinking even before you think it.

LYSANDER: Really? And what am I thinking?

LEON: You're thinking about a woman. A lovely woman who cares very much for you. A woman you've left behind.

LYSANDER: Huh?

LEON: Laura.

LYSANDER: How dare you…

LEON: I'm only saying –

[Lysander strikes Leon.]

LYSANDER: She's not to be mentioned, you hear? Not ever, not again.

LEON: Christ, you're in a mood.

LYSANDER: I'm in whatever mood I please. There'll be no words here for or about Laura. Understand?

LEON: … what are you going to do with her, then?

LYSANDER: Shut up.

LEON: You have to do something. You can't have three women.

LYSANDER: I can have as many women as I like. Anyway, the only woman I really have is Marcia. She's my love.

LEON: And Laura…?

LYSANDER: L doesn't count. She's over. In the past. Done with.

LEON: I don't know if she'd see it that way.

LYSANDER: Enough!

LEON: …What are you going to do, then?

LYSANDER: About what?

LEON: The letter.

LYSANDER: Oh. This. Well, it's clear.

LEON: Yes?

LYSANDER: Tonight I must be with Felicia. She wrote the letter. The least I can do is answer it, right?

LEON: And your true heart?

LYSANDER: It can wait. Come on. Let's see where this St. James Street is.

[Lysander and Leon exit. Felicia appears.]

FELICIA: You'll find it soon enough.
Oh Lysander, you're falling for me.
You will fall.
And Marcia's sweet little love won't be enough to rescue you.
I can love anyone.
I can be as cruel as Don Juan.
Because that's how he wants me.

[Exits.]

Scene 4

[Gerry enters.]

GERRY: And here I am, the forgotten one,

The abandoned one.
Name's Gerry. You might have heard of me.
I'm the one nobody notices.
The quiet type in the corner.
The one people pass over at parties and the like.
The good man who's often mistaken for a fool
Just because he doesn't have the right answers all the time.
I'm the unseen lover.
And I'm not even masked.
Marcia can't see me. She won't.
She's forgotten me.
Although at one time, she used to say
"Gerry, how I love you."
I thought she meant it. She must've, right?
I'd never known Marcia to be untrue.
But one day, without warning,
She said "Goodbye." Just like that.
Well, you can guess the rest. Broken heart, that's me.
Love-struck, love-dumb.
I followed her here. Just to see her.
I'm right out of a book. That's the truth.
But what else can I do?
I have to tell my story.
I have to see it through.

[Marcia appears at the window briefly.]

There she is now.
Marcia! Dear Marcia!

[She withdraws.]

Oh, let me look at you again,
Because before your fierce eyes
You will soon see your dear Gerry die.

[Exit.]

Scene 5

[Laura enters. She sings a "sunny" song of heartbreak.]

"Wreck love"

LAURA: When in bloom, love awakes
A sad and sadder day.
It destroys and it breaks
And puts me in a state.
Love, love, you wreck me,
Like a spider (trapped) in a maze.
Love, love, you wound me,
And I'll never be the same.
When consumed, love despairs
A sad and sadder glare.
It debates and it dares
And ceases all repair.
Love, love, you wreck me
Like a spider in a-
FELIX: *(enters, out of breath)* What is it now, Laura?
LAURA: What?
FELIX: Are you okay?

LAURA: I'll die. That's all.

FELIX: What are you talking about?

LAURA: What else would I be talking about, Felix?

FELIX: Love.

LAURA: Love. Exactly, dear Felix (although sometimes you remind me of someone else…No, that can't be). Ruinous, ridiculous love.

FELIX: Who is it again?

LAURA: Lysander. Lysander!

FELIX: Oh. Right.

LAURA: I'm in love with him. Remember?

FELIX: Yes, of course.

LAURA: I'm in love…

FELIX: Well, that's a good thing, isn't it?

LAURA: No, it's awful.

FELIX: I'm confused.

LAURA: He promised he'd marry me.

FELIX: Yes?

LAURA: And then after we made love, he disappeared.

FELIX: Where'd he go?

LAURA: How should I know?

FELIX: Well, that's men for you.

LAURA: Don't say that, Felix. You're a man.

FELIX: Which is why I can say that. I know all too well.

LAURA: He gave me his word as a husband.

He was so sweet, so warm,

And now, if he does stop by, he just says

"Laura, I'm going to bed,"

And he doesn't even ask me why I'm sad or anything.

And if I text him and ask him where he is,
He doesn't answer. He ignores me.
And if I seek him out to touch him again,
He toys with me,
And makes me beg for his affection;
And then he sleeps with me,
And tells me how much Marcia adores him,
While he's in bed with me!
And I say to him, "Lysander, what about me?"
And he says, "Goodnight, Laura."
FELIX: He's a case all right.
LAURA: I don't understand him. I don't understand anything. My life's a mess. Look at the state I'm in.
FELIX: Singing.
LAURA: Yes. Singing! And you know how I get when I sing?
FELIX: Sad, lonely songs.
LAURA: Miserable heartbreak.
FELIX: Well, maybe it's all for the best.
LAURA: The best? Are you crazy?
FELIX: You know, sometimes with suffering comes great joy.
LAURA: What's that?
FELIX: A saying.
LAURA: Well, it's absurd. Joy from suffering? Must be some kind of perverse joke.
FELIX: I've heard it's true.
LAURA: Don't believe everything you hear. That's a sure way to end up face down in the river.
FELIX: What river?
LAURA: It's an expression.

FELIX: Well, I'm only quoting…

LAURA: And what am I…? I'm living on bits of words and promises…He was supposed to be here tonight.

FELIX: Who?

LAURA: Lysander. Lysander!

FELIX: Oh. So, he re-appeared?

LAURA: In a manner of speaking. He sent word he'd be here tonight. I was so excited. I got a new dress and perfume, And I went to that fabulous salon you like so much – See? They did my hair.

FELIX: It's very pretty.

LAURA: It was very pretty. But after eight hours… I'm afraid it's not much of anything. Where the hell is he?

FELIX: Well, all I know is it's three o' clock and you're wide awake.

LAURA: I can't sleep. I can't eat. I can't do anything I can't stand it when I'm like this.

FELIX: It's love.

LAURA: It's madness. I'm better off dead.

FELIX: Don't say such things.

LAURA: I am. At least my suffering would be at an end. No more Lysander to think about, dream about, cry over…

FELIX: Now, now, no tears. I won't have them.

LAURA: But I want to cry. I want to cry rivers and oceans And swamps and gullies and everything else that's watery…

FELIX: Calm down.

LAURA: I can't. Lysander won't let me. Every time I try to rub him out of my mind, he comes back to me like a damned ghost.

FELIX: Well, cry, then, if that's what you want.

LAURA: That's exactly what I want.

FELIX: Have a good long cry.

LAURA: I will. I will cry….Dammit.

FELIX: That's the spirit.

LAURA: Screw Lysander!

FELIX: Screw him.

LAURA: May he rot in hell and all its circles.

FELIX: May he meet his Maker and find no mercy on judgment day.

LAURA: Oh, Felix, I'm so lucky to have you.

FELIX: Yes, you are.

LAURA: You're so good to me.

FELIX: I love you.

LAURA: …You always have, haven't you?

FELIX: Ever since we met.

LAURA: That day in the park.

FELIX: You were wearing a yellow dress.

LAURA: You remember?

FELIX: I remember everything. Yellow with a soft collar and the most delicious pair of shoes.

LAURA: My Italian shoes!

FELIX: Were they?

LAURA: I always wore them with that dress.

FELIX: They were something. You were something.

LAURA: And now I'm a sorry excuse for a woman.

FELIX: No, you still are something. You must need to figure some things out, that's all.

LAURA: Oh, Felix… dear, dear Felix… You must think I'm awful.

FELIX: I don't.

LAURA: You should. I don't give you anything.

FELIX: You give me enough.

LAURA: Scraps.

FELIX: Tears.

LAURA: Death.

FELIX: Stop that.

LAURA: I'd rather die. It'd be better for everyone.

FELIX: Not for me.

LAURA: Especially for you. After all you've put up with, my death would be a very sweet end.

FELIX: Stop. This instant. I'm the one who's going to put an end to all this.

LAURA: What do you mean?

FELIX: Lysander. He has no right to treat you badly and get away with it. I'll go after him myself

LAURA: At this hour?

FELIX: At whatever hour.

LAURA: You'd do that for me?

FELIX: I would and I will.

LAURA: Oh, Felix, you're an angel.

FELIX: I'm what I have to be.

LAURA: Wait. Are you sure you want to do this?

FELIX: I'd like nothing better than to find Lysander and get this night over with for once and for all.

LAURA: A kiss, then. For luck.

[She kisses him.]

FELIX: ….I don't know what to say.
LAURA: Say you'll find him. For my sake.
FELIX: I'll find him….if it's the last thing I do…

[Felix walks away. Laura is alone.]

LAURA: Oh, Lysander, look what you've done now.
You've taken dear Felix away from me.
Rotten Lysander. Silly Lysander. Lovely Lysander.
Let my eyes surrender to yours…
And may you find your own exquisite death in time.

[Laura exits.]

Scene 6

[Felicia, followed by Don Juan.]

DON JUAN: You're in a hurry. Where are you off to?
FELICIA: It's no concern of yours.
DON JUAN: Everything you do concerns me.
FELICIA: Is that so?
DON JUAN: You know, I may be Don Juan, but I'm not inhuman.
FELICIA: You're a figment.
DON JUAN: I thought I was flesh and blood.
FELICIA: A carnal catastrophe.
DON JUAN: You delight in wounding me, don't you?
FELICIA: I'm glad my words have an effect. Yes.
DON JUAN: Look, Felicia, stop this little game.
What's Lysander to you?

FELICIA: Marcia's lover.

DON JUAN: Exactly. So, why go after him when you have me?

FELICIA: First of all, I'm not going after him.
I don't go after men. And secondly, how do I know I have you?

DON JUAN: Because from this moment on, I'll be true.

FELICIA: Another song.

DON JUAN: My eyes belong to Felicia and only to Felicia.

FELICIA: You don't tire of this dance, do you?

DON JUAN: I'll never tire of you.

FELICIA: Are you proposing to me?

DON JUAN: I don't believe in marriage. You know that.

FELICIA: Then what do you want from me? Just tireless love until eternity without commitment of any kind?

DON JUAN: Something like that.

FELICIA: You know, for a moment, I actually thought you were serious.

DON JUAN: I was. I am. Can't you see?

FELICIA: What I see is a spoiled boy who only wants his spoils. Well, sorry.

DON JUAN: Wait.

FELICIA: What now?

DON JUAN: …What does Lysander offer you?

FELICIA: At the moment he offers me more than you.

DON JUAN: Which is?

FELICIA: Faith. Trust. Blind courage.

DON JUAN: All that?

FELICIA: He doesn't know me. Not really, and yet he'll see me on my terms. Without question.

DON JUAN: He's quite a sport.

FELICIA: He's a gambler.

DON JUAN: The pattern repeats itself.

FELICIA: Which pattern is that?

DON JUAN: The pattern of men you fall for.

FELICIA: So, now I've a pattern?

DON JUAN: We all do.

FELICIA: Am I part of your pattern, then?

DON JUAN: No. You're different.

FELICIA: Should I be flattered?

DON JUAN: Maybe.

FELICIA: What do I inspire in you, Don Juan?

DON JUAN: Fear.

FELICIA: …I'm not sure what you mean.

DON JUAN: Don't play coy with me. We're past that game.

FELICIA: You twist everything around.

DON JUAN: Do I?

FELICIA: Yes.

DON JUAN: We're even, then.

FELICIA: …I want Lysander for Lysander.

DON JUAN: And nothing more?

FELICIA: Nothing at all.

DON JUAN: Seek him out.

FELICIA: I don't need your blessing.

DON JUAN: You have it anyway.

FELICIA: Really?

DON JUAN: Absolutely.

FELICIA: And yet a moment ago…

DON JUAN: I know. But people change.

FELICIA: Not in a moment.

DON JUAN: Sometimes in seconds. You'd be surprised. Human beings have an amazing potentiality.

FELICIA: I won't see him, then.

DON JUAN: As you wish.

FELICIA: Not as I wish. As you wish.

DON JUAN: What riddle is this?

FELICIA: What kind of fool do you take me for?

DON JUAN: Love's fool.

FELICIA: Give me your gun.

DON JUAN: High drama now?

FELICIA: The highest.

DON JUAN: I'm afraid I don't have it on me.

FELICIA: What about your dagger?

DON JUAN: What about it?

FELICIA: Lose that too?

DON JUAN: No.

FELICIA: Give it, then.

DON JUAN: What for?

FELICIA: A little blood-letting.

DON JUAN: Finally…

FELICIA: Ready to meet your end?

DON JUAN: Oh. Yes.

…

What are you waiting for, love?

I'm here. I'm ready.

FELICIA: …No.

DON JUAN: Changed your mind?

FELICIA: I don't know what I'm doing.
DON JUAN: You're going to kill me so you can run off with Lysander.
FELICIA: No.
DON JUAN: You're not going to kill me?
FELICIA: No.
DON JUAN: Pity. I was so looking forward to your being my last vision on earth.
FELICIA: Why do you do this?
DON JUAN: Do what?
FELICIA: You know perfectly well.
DON JUAN: Everything I do, dear, is out of love.

[He reveals a small jewelry box.]

FELICIA: …What's that?
DON JUAN: Just a little something I picked up. Take it.
FELICIA: …No.
DON JUAN: I'll force your love.
FELICIA: You'll do nothing of the kind. Go on, find someone else. Charm another woman.
DON JUAN: I don't want to.
FELICIA: Lost your touch?
DON JUAN: I don't want anyone else, Felicia.
FELICIA: Well, you should've thought of that when you went off with what's-their-names that night.
DON JUAN: If you go off with Lysander, you'll pay for it.
FELICIA: Are you threatening me?
DON JUAN: Only speaking true.

FELICIA: I think I liked you better when you were in your lying mood.
DON JUAN: Give a kiss. Don't be so resentful towards me. I don't deserve it.

[She kisses him. He returns it.]

See how easy this is, love? We can just stay here like this forever.
FELICIA: …No.
DON JUAN: Felicia…
FELICIA: Lysander's expecting me.
DON JUAN: True to your word, eh?
FELICIA: It's all I have.

[Felicia exits.]

ACT TWO, Scene 7

[Marcia appears, alone.]

MARCIA: I'm brave and cowardly,
Cruel and merciful,
Reasonable yet mad.
This is how I am now.
This is how I spend my days,
yearning for the night,
And yet as soon as it arrives,
I wish nothing more but for it to end,
And end now – at once - immediately.

But it doesn't end.
It goes on, and I'm at its mercy.
I'm consumed, you see?
With what? I couldn't say.
Is this love? Madness?
All I know is my life is misery
Ever since Lysander walked into it.
It's as if my will has escaped me,
And I'm ruled only by desire,
A desire that knows no direction and no bounds.
I just want, and want,
And I don't even know what I want.
Pleasure and displeasure are to be found
in equal measure,
And I crave them both indiscriminately.
I crave everything,
And do nothing but wait
For his voice, his face, his eyes
To tell me who I am.
What's happening to me?

[Laura appears]

LAURA: You're in love.
MARCIA: What?
LAURA: You're not yourself when you're in love. I know all about that, Marcia. Believe me.
MARCIA: And you are…?
LAURA: Laura. You don't know me. We run in different circles. I'm from a good family, though. Not like yours, of course-

MARCIA: No. Of course not. That's a nice dress, though.

LAURA: Not as pretty as yours.

MARCIA: No. It couldn't possibly be. Mine was especially made.

LAURA: Really? I didn't know people still did that.

MARCIA: Oh. All the time. It's the only way to remain fashion forward.

LAURA: Really?

MARCIA: Yes. You know… Your eyes are so…

LAURA: What? What's wrong with my eyes?

LAURA: Nothing. They're…bewitching, that's all.

LAURA: You flatter me. It's your beauty that overwhelms me.

MARCIA: Have we met before?

LAURA: Only in passing. But we've much in common.

MARCIA: And what's that?

LAURA: Love.

MARCIA: Love or its object?

LAURA: I shouldn't say.

MARCIA: Say.

LAURA: Well, if you must know –

MARCIA: I don't know if it's a question of "must," but since you're here, staring at me like that, I'd certainly like to know.

LAURA: Well, you see I've been seeing someone for quite some time. Actually, even before you've been seeing this person,

MARCIA: Before I…?

LAURA: Or anyone else, for that matter, has been
seeing him.
MARCIA: Him? This person is someone we both
know?
LAURA: I don't presume that you know him in the
same way that I do – I mean, if we're to use the word
"know" in the Biblical sense.
MARCIA: You're charming.
LAURA: I'm just trying to be polite.
MARCIA: Well, if this person is the person I think we
both know, then let's not be polite at all, but say
exactly what's on our mind.
LAURA: Are you sure?
MARCIA: You come to me as a friend?
LAURA: Yes.
MARCIA: Then let's be friends. Let's be absolutely
frank with each other.
LAURA: Even if what I'll say will upset you?
MARCIA: I'd rather be upset than ignorant.
LAURA: Very well, then… Your Lysander was
promised to me before you two even met.
MARCIA: What?
LAURA: We'd been promised for quite some time.
In fact, I was sure he'd marry me. He said as much.
But then one day he left my bed
And I didn't know where he went.
I tried to follow him but he was too quick for me.
I tried writing but he won't answer my letters.
He's been avoiding me, you see?
And I don't know why.
Well, I do know why, but I didn't know at first,

And now that I know it's you –
I can forgive him a little,
Because well, you're... you're beautiful
and a good person, obviously...
but the fact of the matter is...
Lysander's been rotten to both of us.

MARCIA: Meaning?

LAURA: He's been seeing your friend all this time.

MARCIA: My friend? What friend?

LAURA: And quite regularly, I might add.

MARCIA: Who's he been seeing?

LAURA: Felicia. Of course.

MARCIA: Felicia?

LAURA: I'm sorry to be the one to spill the beans, but it's true. I've seen it with my own eyes.

MARCIA: ...I knew it.

LAURA: You did?

MARCIA: I didn't know for sure, but I know how she operates.

LAURA: And him. He's been operating too! It's not right.

MARCIA: No. But Felicia...

LAURA: Look, I know you love him – I love him too –And I know we find it hard to find fault in those we love, but – he's a real shit. Admit it.

MARCIA: He's a shit.

LAURA: That's right.

MARCIA: He's a rotten, putrid, smelly shit.

LAURA: That's the spirit.

MARCIA: He's the worst shit on the effing planet and I'll make him pay for every lousy, double-crossing thing he's ever done!

LAURA: Well said!

MARCIA: But I don't like saying it.

LAURA: Because your heart is full of him. But you have to see Lysander clearly for once and for all. Because if you don't… he'll go on treating both of us like this. And if he marries Felicia,

MARCIA: Marries her?

LAURA: There's been talk of that.

MARCIA: I don't believe it.

LAURA: Believe it.

MARCIA: But he's supposed to marry me.

LAURA: Actually, he's supposed to marry me.

MARCIA: Oh God. This is a mess.

LAURA: That's why I came to see you. I thought if we could…

MARCIA: Do something?

LAURA: Yes.

MARCIA: We should. Definitely. Do something.

LAURA: But what?

MARCIA: I don't know. I can't think. My mind is… Lysander's such a shit!

LAURA: I know.

MARCIA: I mean, how could he possibly think he could get away with -? Two women?

LAURA: Three.

MARCIA: What are we going to do?

LAURA: You could say we're related.

MARCIA: What'd you mean?

LAURA: Well, I don't want him to know I'm here. The thought of him knowing I crawled all the way over here to find him and you is too pitiful, really.

MARCIA: You crawled?

LAURA: No. Just a figure of speech.

MARCIA: Oh, I was worried for a minute there. I mean, no one, and I mean, no one should crawl for love.

LAURA: Absolutely. Just say we're cousins and that you're letting me stay awhile.

MARCIA: Cousins it is.

LAURA: Thank you, Marcia.

MARCIA: No need to thank me. We've both been wronged in love.

LAURA: I know. It makes me sick. Sick sick sick….

MARCIA: Now now, we mustn't let anger or despair get the best of us. That's exactly what they want. What we have to do is act with intelligence and speed.

LAURA: I like the sound of that.

MARCIA: Let's plan our revenge.

LAURA: Revenge!

MARCIA: Once we execute it, we''ll be merciless, not sweet.

[They exit.]

Scene 8

[Lysander enters reading a text from Laura on his phone. Leon follows him.]

LEON: So, L's going into a convent?

LYSANDER: So it seems.

LEON: That's extreme.

LYSANDER: L can expend her energies on prayer and devotion, instead of writing these ridiculous texts and hounding me all over the city like she does now.

LEON: You're such an asshole.

LYSANDER: I've my limits, okay? You want me to be a saint? L's passion for me is pointless. Haven't I told her with my actions alone – forget my words –that I don't care for her anymore?

LEON: But you did once.

LYSANDER: Yes, I did; I did, of course, but things are different now.

LEON: Because you've Felicia.

LYSANDER: And Marcia. Don't forget.

LEON: You'll end up with neither.

LYSANDER: What's that?

LEON: You can't have them both.

LYSANDER: Why not? I can marry Marcia and keep Felicia on the side.

LEON: I don't believe you.

LYSANDER: It's not unheard of. Governor Winston did…

LEON: Governor Winston was a terrible statesman and by all accounts, a pretty miserable human being. How could you possibly look up to-?

LYSANDER: Leon, monogamy is a myth. It's an impossible myth. Men aren't expected to…

LEON: Be decent human beings?

LYSANDER: Look who's talking…

LEON: Hey. I don't shit all over people, okay? I'm straight up. Honest.

LYSANDER: And so am I. What I'm proposing is a perfectly honest deal.

LEON: Yeah? And what would Marcia say about it? I mean, you're an honest man, right? So, you would tell her?

LYSANDER: I hadn't thought about that.

LEON: Think again, dude, before you screw everything up.

LYSANDER: I won't screw anything up. Don't you have faith in me?

LEON: I don't know anymore.

LYSANDER: I'll figure something out.

LEON: You better.

LYSANDER: I will. Right now I just…. I don't want to think about it.

LEON: Cause you're having your cake…

LYSANDER: Yeah, yeah…One thing's clear, though.

LEON: What's that?

LYSANDER: Marcia's the one. She's the one for me.

LEON: You are so fucked.

LYSANDER: I'm not.

LEON: What about Felicia? What's she?

LYSANDER: Felicia is…fun. You know. Good fun.

LEON: And Laura?

[Lysander strikes Leon]

LYSANDER: What did I tell you, eh? What did I tell you? Not one more word about L, you hear? L is off limits, not to be mentioned, *finito!* You hear me?

LEON: …Yes.

[Lysander stops hitting him.]

LYSANDER: I've had enough of L. That's all you ever want to talk about. What is it? You want her or something?

LEON: No.

LYSANDER: Are you sure? You're not secretly pining?

LEON: What's it to you? You don't love her anymore.

LYSANDER: No, but that doesn't mean…You can't have her. Understand?

LEON: What?

LYSANDER: You can't.

LEON: Why not?

LYSANDER: I won't allow it.

LEON: I can do what I want.

[Lysander strikes him.]

LYSANDER: You want to work for me?
You want to keep earning your pretty little check?
Then lay off… stay away from L.
She's nothing to you. You hear? You hear me?

LEON: Yeah. Yeah.

LYSANDER: Good.

LEON: …Why do you hit me?

LYSANDER: Huh?

LEON: You hit me all the time.

LYSANDER: I do not.

LEON: You just did.

LYSANDER: Love tap.

LEON: That was not a love tap.

LYSANDER: You can't even take a punch now? You're getting soft.

LEON: I won't put up with this.

LYSANDER: Run away, then. Isn't that what you're good at? You ran away from home, right?

LEON: Don't be such an ass, all right. That's got nothing to do with anything.

LYSANDER: You run. You run away from anything that rings remotely of responsibility.

LEON: When do I do that?

LYSANDER: All the time. Who was it? Brenda?

LEON: That wasn't going to work out anyway.

LYSANDER: How do you know? You didn't even give it time. You ran away. I don't run. I may do what I do as screwed up as it is, according to you, but I don't run. And don't even mention L. Cause that was an entirely different story. Come on. Rub my feet.

LEON: The things I do…

LYSANDER: The things we all do…

LEON: So, what are you going to do?

LYSANDER: About what?

LEON: The text.

LYSANDER: What text?

LEON: You know. L.

LYSANDER: Oh. Well, there's only one thing to do.

[Lysander smashes his phone. Felicia enters.]

FELICIA: Is that what you do with love?
LYSANDER: Felicia. I was just about to –

[Felicia strikes Lysander.]

FELICIA: You're worse than all the rest of them put together!
LYSANDER: What did I do?
FELICIA: What didn't you do?
LYSANDER: Look, honey, whatever it is I can explain…
FELICIA: Explain what?
LYSANDER: The text, the phone…
FELICIA: Yes.
LYSANDER: It's from…She's from my past. I'm sure you understand.
FELICIA: And this is the way you treat your past? You destroy it?
LYSANDER: She's nothing to you. In fact, you're the reason I'm breaking my word to God and the world.
FELICIA: Don't bring God into this, you little hypocrite.
LYSANDER: Look, Felicia, I don't know what's gotten into you, But everything's fine. Haven't I sworn my love to you over and over again? Haven't I given you everything you've asked? I love you, okay? I love you, and you alone.
FELICIA: You mean that?
LYSANDER: Yes.

FELICIA: I want to believe you.
LYSANDER: Then do.
FELICIA: Oh, Lysander…

[*She embraces Lysander. A moment.*]

LYSANDER: What's wrong?
FELICIA: Are we friends?
LYSANDER: More than friends.
FELICIA: But friends first, yes?
LYSANDER: If you value friendship so highly, then yes, friends first.
FELICIA: And Marcia? Is she your friend?
LYSANDER: Stop.
FELICIA: And what about this other woman, this… from your past?
LYSANDER: For God's sake!
FELICIA: I want to believe you, Lysander. I do. But how can I believe you if I don't trust you?
…
LYSANDER: You have my word. As a friend and a lover. I am true…. To you.
FELICIA: The way you say things…
LYSANDER: I mean them.
FELICIA: I know you do. I just don't know what to do…
LYSANDER: Do what you will with me. I'm yours. Completely.
FELICIA: …I'm going to the park tonight. Will you wait for me?
LYSANDER: It's a big park.

FELICIA: You'll find me.

LYSANDER: Where?

FELICIA: In the orchard.

LYSANDER: What about the party in old town?

FELICIA: We'll see each other. In the park.

LYSANDER: Wherever you wish. I'm yours. You know that.

FELICIA: We'll see. Now, go on. Leave me be.

LYSANDER: Come along, Leon.

LEON: And not a moment too soon.

[Lysander and Leon exit. Felicia remains.]

FELICIA: I can love him. I can love anybody.
But I'm not a slave to love. That's where he's wrong.
I do what I want with love.
I toy with it, I flirt with it, I let it fill me, I banish it.
Love is my servant. Not the other way around.
Cursed be the woman who loves only one man.
It's selfish to limit yourself to a single lover.
Although I admit Lysander does tempt me
To consider the possibility.
But I won't. I can't. Love's too big
To give to one person and one person only.
It should be divided equally among many.
Let me have a million lovers. They'll never have me.

Scene 9

[Gerry enters, out of breath.]

GERRY: Even if they want you?

FELICIA: Gerry? What are you doing here? (It is Gerry, right?)

GERRY: Yeah. It is. The one and the same. Oh, Felicia, I don't know. To tell you the truth, I've been wandering about aimlessly ever since Marcia left me.

FELICIA: Poor Gerry.

GERRY: Don't pity me, please.

FELICIA: You're enjoying your suffering?

GERRY: It's all I have. Might as well revel in it.

FELICIA: You're wasting your time. You know that.

GERRY: She adores Lysander. I know.

FELICIA: So, why carry on in this loveless limbo when you can have me?

GERRY: What are you saying?

FELICIA: Only that I love you, that I could love you, that I'd love to love you freely.

GERRY: Stop. Please.

FELICIA: You don't believe me?

GERRY: I believe you don't know what you want; so you chase after everything madly, without a thought in your head.

FELICIA: My thinking is quite clear.

GERRY: I love Marcia. Understand?

FELICIA: But she doesn't love you. So, what do you gain in living a life of emptiness and solitude and worthless pining?

GERRY: My love for Marcia keeps me alive.

FELICIA: You're a wreck.

GERRY: And you have no feelings.

FELICIA: You're wrong.

GERRY: Really? You'd betray Marcia just like that?

FELICIA: I don't understand.

GERRY: You're her friend, and yet you offer yourself to me – her former lover?…I'm out of here..

FELICIA: Wait! Gerry!

GERRY: I'd rather have my loveless love than anything you can give me.

[Gerry exits]

FELICIA: Oh, now I'm going to have to follow him…or someone else. Cupid, if you exist, give me strength, for clearly everyone seeks my end.

DON JUAN: *(appears)* Not everyone.

FELICIA: Leave me alone, Don Juan.

DON JUAN: Confounded in love, are you?

FELICIA: Never.

DON JUAN: First Lysander, then Gerry, then…who will it be next?

FELICIA: Not you.

DON JUAN: You're jealous and confused. I like you like this.

FELICIA: I don't understand how you can possibly spend every waking moment thinking about me. You must be quite bored, Don Juan, to obsess about my heart endlessly.

DON JUAN: Who says I obsess?

FELICIA: I can see it.

DON JUAN: Actually, I've stopped thinking about you. Really. I've realized that you could never love me.

FELICIA: Why's that?

DON JUAN: You don't believe in the epic.

FELICIA: Spare me the drama.

DON JUAN: But, honey, we're in one.

FELICIA: Last I checked this was a comedy.

DON JUAN: Comedies about love are always tinged with tragedy.

FELICIA: Philosophize all you want.

DON JUAN: There is more in heaven and earth, my dear Felicia, than mere philosophy.

FELICIA: Epic? Epic? You don't know the meaning of it.

DON JUAN: After several operas and countless plays, I think I do.

FELICIA: Don Juan of legend.

DON JUAN: And Felicia's story…

FELICIA: Has gone unwritten.

DON JUAN: Until now.

FELICIA: Yes. But if you insist on rewriting it-

DON JUAN: I don't insist, dear one, but you talk and talk about love, but in the end, you settle for stupid little adventures. Insignificant affairs. Sad, really. I thought once we were equal.

FELICIA: We are.

DON JUAN: I would never throw myself at Gerry.

FELICIA: Really? I seem to remember a scene or two in a distant draft…

DON JUAN: That scene was cut.

FELICIA: Because Gerry wasn't to your liking?

DON JUAN: Now, now, Felicia…

FELICIA: What is it, Don Juan?

DON JUAN: Let's not get carried away.

FELICIA: But I want to. I so want to.

DON JUAN: Felicia.

FELICIA: Oh. Yes. Yes. Yes!

DON JUAN: Felicia!

FELICIA: *(dryly)* What?

DON JUAN: Please. We have to keep this respectable.

FELICIA: Why?

DON JUAN: There are children in the audience.

FELICIA: Didn't they read the sign?

DON JUAN: What sign?

FELICIA: "Mature themes."

DON JUAN: You know no one reads those signs.

FELICIA: Precisely. So, why be respectable when we can be… *(she advances passionately)*

DON JUAN: Felicia…. Okay, okay, okay. Stop! …You see this is exactly what I mean.

FELICIA: About what?

DON JUAN: About you with…with Gerry…throwing yourself.

FELICIA: Are we back to that again? Listen, honey, I was not throwing myself.

DON JUAN: What were you doing?

FELICIA: I was trying to talk to him, to make him see reason. Poor thing, he's drowning in love.

DON JUAN: I think Gerry's rather noble.

FELICIA: What's with you all of a sudden?

DON JUAN: Hmm?

FELICIA: Caring, philosophizing….making pronouncements?

DON JUAN: I'm a caring fellow.

FELICIA: You're a scoundrel. Nothing more.

DON JUAN: I miss you, Felicia. See, this is what happens when a man misses his true love. He becomes someone else. He loses his way.

FELICIA: And if I came back to you?

DON JUAN: I'd be reborn.

FELICIA: Mighty resurrection.

DON JUAN: I'd astonish the world.

FELICIA: But what could you give me?

DON JUAN: 'Never a dull moment.'

FELICIA: And…?

DON JUAN: What more do you want?

FELICIA: Constancy.

DON JUAN: Don't kid yourself. The last thing in the world that you want is a constant lover.

FELICIA: That's where you're wrong.

DON JUAN: Really? So, you think Gerry, Lysander….? By the way, how is Lysander?

FELICIA: What'd you mean?

DON JUAN: As a lover?

FELICIA: I'm not going to discuss this with you.

DON JUAN: If we're nothing to each other, then why not discuss things as friends?

FELICIA: We're not friends.

DON JUAN: What are we, then?

FELICIA: Strange attractors.

DON JUAN: I think my strangeness has rubbed off on you.

FELICIA: I've always been like this.

DON JUAN: Sad case.

FELICIA: No sadder than you.

DON JUAN: What do you make of this Lysander? You think he'll marry you?

FELICIA: As a matter of fact, yes. I think he will.

DON JUAN: It's serious, then?

FELICIA: I don't play games anymore.

DON JUAN: Without games, there's nothing to love.

FELICIA: Without games, there's more to love.

DON JUAN: More and more and more. That's what you want.

FELICIA: …Going to the party in old town?

DON JUAN: I might.

FELICIA: Maybe I'll see you there, then.

DON JUAN: Watch yourself.

FELICIA: What's that?

DON JUAN: Don't forget to have a good time on my account.

FELICIA: Oh, I will. Don't you worry.

[She exits.]

DON JUAN: I'll die a thousand deaths before you get what you want, Felicia.

[He exits.]

Scene 10

[Marcia and Laura enter]

MARCIA: Lysander is drowning in the Felician sea.

LAURA: But when oh when will he come back to me?

MARCIA: Don't cry. These things take time. You won't be lost for long, if I can help it.

LAURA: I know. I trust you, but it seems awfully cruel that Lysander thinks it's you. He's talking to every night outside your window, when it's really me.

MARCIA: You enjoy talking to him, don't you?

LAURA: Yes.

MARCIA: Then don't worry. He won't be disappointed to find out it's you. And heaven knows he deserves to be lied to after the way he's treated both of us. Actually, I'm more concerned about Gerry right now....He hasn't come by in quite some time. I don't know what's happening. He adores me; he's never stopped adoring me until now.

LAURA: Maybe he's finally awakened to your rejection.

MARCIA: No. No. I know Gerry. He sings to me, He does, He serenades me. So old-skool. He's sweet, really. Because you'd think after seven years, he'd get tired of...But he's been quite good 'til now.

LAURA: Maybe you should sing to him.

MARCIA: What I should do is love him. Now that Lysander has deceived me so openly; There's room in my heart for Gerry. We must find him before he gives up on me completely. Oh Laura, I'm so glad we met,

LAURA: I only wish the circumstances had been different.

MARCIA: Come, let's seek our destinies before they catch up with us.

[They exit.]

Scene 11

[Don Juan enters, followed by Felix.]

DON JUAN: Felix, she was in the park, as I suspected.
FELIX: You know everything, Don Juan.
DON JUAN: I'm afraid only God knows everything. I can only know what gossip and my eyes can tell me.
FELIX: But it was Felicia. You're sure of it?
DON JUAN: With Lysander.
FELIX: I will kill him!
DON JUAN: Now, now, don't go crazy on me.
FELIX: But he's betrayed my Laura. What else should I do but seek his death?
DON JUAN: Believe me, there are other ways to get revenge, or have you forgotten my love for Felicia?
FELIX: No. No, this must be hard for you, too.
DON JUAN: Well, it's not easy; let's put it that way.
FELIX: So, you saw them, then, in the park?
DON JUAN: They were declaring their love for each other. It was quite romantic. Such tender words were coming from their mouths that I thought I'd stumbled onto the wrong couple. I mean, Felicia's a dream, but she's not the tender type. And Lysander...well, I don't know him, but he doesn't strike me as the kind who would go for the hearts-and-flowers delivery. But there they were: all lovey-dovey, like kids making up. It was sweet.
FELIX: What did you do?

DON JUAN: What could I do? I listened. And after they bid their goodbyes, I followed Felicia to her door.

FELIX: And?

DON JUAN: I said hello. And she said "Perfect timing, Don Juan," at which point I decided to take out my dagger and stab her with it.

FELIX: What?

DON JUAN: You heard me.

FELIX: Oh, I'm all for revenge, but I don't want to hurt anybody.

DON JUAN: Don't worry. My arm restrained me.

FELIX: Your arm counseled you properly.

DON JUAN: I slapped her instead.

FELIX: You did what?

DON JUAN: And I left her and went straight to Lysander, who I found, incidentally, sitting inside a church of all places, and I told him everything. So it's all over now.

FELIX: I don't know what to say.

DON JUAN: You could congratulate me.

FELIX: On what? On slapping a woman? No. I won't congratulate you on that. As much as she wrecked things, so did he. Why should Lysander come out all rosy in this picture? It's not right.

DON JUAN: I thought you'd be happy.

FELIX: The last thing I wanted was for you to do my dirty work for me.

DON JUAN: They call it "dirty work" for a reason, Felix.

FELIX: I'll have no part of it.

DON JUAN: Felix! I'm trying you to teach you the ways of the world.
FELIX: The ways of this world are wrong.

[Felix exits. Don Juan remains, puzzled.]

ACT THREE

Scene 12

[Laura enters, alone]

LAURA: I'm consumed with jealousy,
and to what end?
Lysander is Lysander. Felicia is Felicia.
And I'm poor, miserable Laura, and nothing more.
Jealousy does not sleep with me
or pleasure me or give me gifts.
It doesn't write me letters or songs or poems.
And it doesn't divine my future and predict harmonious things.
All jealousy does is ravage and consume
And gnaw at my insides.
It's gotten to the point where
I can't even look at the sky and delight in its beauty.
What good is that? What good is revenge if you can't enjoy it?

[Laura withdraws. Gerry enters, out of breath.]

GERRY: Marcia?

MARCIA: *(appears)* I'm right here.

GERRY: I heard you were here. But I couldn't believe you'd see me.

MARCIA: Of course I'll see you, Gerry. I'm seeing you now, aren't I?

GERRY: After seven years, I pretty much had lost hope that you'd offer me your affection.

MARCIA: You're so sweet. Just like your songs and poems.

GERRY: I wish I had a song for you now, but in truth, I'm a bit at a loss to have you so close to me.

MARCIA: See? That's what I like. A sweet and honest man. No trickery.

GERRY: I'd never lie to you, Marcia.

MARCIA: No, I believe you wouldn't. Come. Kiss me.

GERRY: Now?

MARCIA: What better time is there?

GERRY: I'm afraid…of losing you.

MARCIA: But I'm right here.

GERRY: I'm afraid of losing my happiness.

MARCIA: Gerry. You've won me. Can't you see?

GERRY: I'd rather die than let this moment go, for I fear you'll soon scorn me.

MARCIA: Why would I do that?

GERRY: Because that's all you've done these last seven years.

MARCIA: Don't make me feel guilty, Gerry. I'm trying to do good by you.

GERRY: Good by me? That's not enough.

MARCIA: I'm sorry. That came out wrong. What I mean is…

GERRY: What?

MARCIA: It'd be my honor to be your wife.

GERRY: You mean that?

MARCIA: Absolutely. I'm yours, Gerry, if you'll have me.

GERRY: If I'll have you? Dear Marcia, look at me. Look. What do you see? Is this not the very picture of love staring you in the face? Is this not devotion complete? Beloved wife, may the heavens bless our union and bring us eternal happiness.

MARCIA: I'd settle for earthly happiness, Gerry.

GERRY: Whatever you desire shall be yours, my dear. I'll see to it.

MARCIA: I couldn't ask for anything more than your love.

GERRY: And I yours.

MARCIA: Kiss me.

GERRY: May this day never end.

[They kiss, and then go within.]

Scene 13

[Lysander enters.]

LYSANDER: Everyone's turned against me, and I don't know why. Don Juan says one thing, Felicia says another, Marcia says a third... And all I can think about is L, whom I deceived so grievously and whose curses are surely working their dark magic on me. All I want to do is to love and be loved. Is that so wrong?

And if not love, then at least give me the imitation of it. But this? This is madness beyond madness. All I can do now is talk to Marcia and convince her to be my wife. I see now as I did before that she's the only one for me. Marcia, you rule my destiny. My soul, my life, let me see you again.

[Marcia and Laura appear in obscured view on the terrace. They both wear cloaks.]

Marcia? Is that you, my dear?
LAURA: Not another word, Lysander. I've heard all I need to hear.
LYSANDER: What are you talking about? Marcia…
LAURA: No more lies, my friend. No more tears for me. I don't want to see you ever again. Understand? Goodbye, Lysander.
LYSANDER: Marcia?
LAURA: All I have now is death's sure and faithful company, and his company, and no one else's, is all I seek. Follow your fancy wherever it leads, be it with Felicia or whomever you please. Goodbye, Lysander.
LYSANDER: Wait! Marcia! Don't do this to me.
LAURA: After all you've done? You must be kidding me.
MARCIA: That's enough now. Come on.
LAURA: No. I want to hear what he has to say.
LYSANDER: Marcia, Marcia…
LAURA: Yes?
LYSANDER: Beautiful Marcia, I want to apologize…

LAURA: You're too late, my friend. May the one whom you love best die a slow, wretched death in your arms. You deserve nothing less.

[Laura withdraws.]

LYSANDER: Marcia!

MARCIA: It's no use. Her mind's made up.

LYSANDER: Help me. Please.

MARCIA: I don't know what I could do. I'm only her assistant, sir. I'm not her conscience.

LYSANDER: Her assistant?

MARCIA: Yes.

LYSANDER: When did she hire an assistant?

MARCIA: Oh, you know how it is… things get busy with this, that and the other.

LYSANDER: What kind of things?

MARCIA: It's not my place, sir.

LYSANDER: Please, stop calling me that.

MARCIA: What?

LYSANDER: Sir sir! It makes me feel like an old man.

MARCUA: Well…

LYSANDER: Please, tell me what to do… for the love of God…

MARCIA: Best leave God out of this if you want to get your way.

LYSANDER: Please.

MARCIA: Well, if you want her back…

LYSANDER: More than life itself.

MARCIA: All right. This is what I think you should do.

LYSANDER: Anything. Tell me.

MARCIA: Mind you, I can't promise it will work.

LYSANDER: It doesn't matter. I'll try it. I'll do anything.

MARCIA: Very well. The first thing you need to do is to tell her how much you care for her.

LYSANDER: Yes.

MARCIA: You'll do that?

LYSANDER: Yes. Yes.

MARCIA: Then you must promise to be her husband.

LYSANDER: I promise.

MARCIA: You must write it down in a sworn statement: "I, Lysander, promise, to be your husband"

LYSANDER: "I, Lysander, promise, to be your husband"

MARCIA: "And to never again be treacherous."

LYSANDER: And to never again be treacherous.

MARCIA: "Despite my own desires." Say it.

LYSANDER: Despite my own desires.

MARCIA: Swear this, and she will be yours til eternity.

LYSANDER: I swear.

MARCIA: Come to the door. I will leave it open for you. You can deliver the message to her yourself.

LYSANDER: I owe you my life, dear woman.

MARCIA: Don't owe me anything. Just do this for my friend.

LYSANDER: You have my word.

MARCIA: Good luck.

[Marcia withdraws. Leon appears]

LEON: Ah, there you are. I was looking all over for you.

LYSANDER: Leave me alone, Leon. I've work to do.

LEON: Work? You're going into my line, eh? Working for a living? You'll have a hard time of it with your temper.

LYSANDER: I'm trying to concentrate.

LEON: On what? Felicia? You can forget about her. Rumor has it she married Don Juan last night.

LYSANDER: What?

LEON: That's what they say.

LYSANDER: Why?

LEON: I don't know. I'm only repeating what I heard.

LYSANDER: No, why would she marry him? He doesn't care for her at all.

LEON: Well, maybe they're striking up a marriage of convenience. Or maybe she has something to hide. What difference does it make?

LYSANDER: I love her, Leon.

LEON: You love everybody, except me.

LYSANDER: Stop talking. Stop saying things. I need to think.

LEON: What about?

LYSANDER: Quiet!

LEON: …Have you stopped thinking yet?

LYSANDER: Leon.

LEON: Sorry.

LYSANDER: …Okay, here's what I think. I think Marcia knows about Felicia's betrayal. Clearly, that's why she was in such a state just now.

LEON: What do you care? There are a thousand girls in this city that will gladly have you.

LYSANDER: But she's the only one I love.

LEON: I tell you what, if I help you out, what will you give me?

LYSANDER: Help me in what way?

LEON: Help you out of this unholy mess.

LYSANDER: I'd give you everything I esteem, love and possess.

LEON: Well, I know a woman who gave me a recipe for a magic potion once.

LYSANDER: You're not serious.

LEON: Hear me out.

LYSANDER: Okay. And what did this woman say?

LEON: It's not what she said; it's what this potion does

LYSANDER: What does it do?

LEON: You believe now, don't you?

LYSANDER: Yes, I believe.

LEON: It cures illnesses, heartbreak, misfortune and turns enemies into lovers.

LYSANDER: I'll take it.

LEON: Hold on now. You have to follow the proper procedure.

LYSANDER: What's that?

LEON: Take a spider's heart that's been dried up by the sun and was extracted during a crescent moon, add liquid from the lake where Echo was turned into a hermaphrodite, stir in some ancient blood and the sad complaints of nightingales and preserve it all with the hairs of a couple of frogs.

LYSANDER: What?

LEON: Then when your love's forgotten you, apply this salve on your forehead or on your belly button and voila! No more pain.

LYSANDER: I'm going to kill you. Do you hear me?

LEON: I guess there's no chance, then, of snagging all that you possess?

LYSANDER: Get away from me or I'll tear you to limb from limb.

LEON: You don't have to tell me twice. I know your fury all too well.

[Leon exits. Marcia, cloaked, appears.]

MARCIA: Psst. Lysander.

LYSANDER: My compass, is that you?

MARCIA: Write your letter. Hurry.

LYSANDER: ·You're my savior.

MARCIA: You haven't much time.

[Lysander withdraws. Marcia remains.]

Oh, Laura will be your wife. You'll pay for your deceit, Lysander, and you'll pay for it dearly.

[Marcia exits.]

Scene 14

[Felicia enters.]

FELICIA: It's been three days
since I've heard from Lysander.
Don Juan has gone off with someone else.
And where am I? Alone. Right back where I started.
I'll kill them all. I've no choice.
If Love asks for revenge, I'll do its bidding.
Love may be my servant, but when it comes to justice,
I'm her slave.
Why should I be condemned for loving as I please?
I'm only an instrument of love.
My heart takes everyone in:
the ugly and the handsome,
The young and the old, the rich and the poor.
Why, if I were a man, I'd be declared a saint
And people would be praying to me
and bringing me offerings.
But because I am a woman,
I am cast off into love's inferno.
Well, I'll have none of it.
My pleasure is mine;
My body is mine,
My soul is mine
And I'll do with it as I choose.
No one has the right to judge me.

Scene 15

[Don Juan appears.]

DON JUAN: Not even me?

FELICIA: Get out of here.

DON JUAN: I just arrived.

FELICIA: You take one more step towards me and I'll take your life.

DON JUAN: Dagger in hand?

FELICIA: My arm is at the ready.

DON JUAN: You wouldn't dare.

FELICIA: Test me.

DON JUAN: I'm not in the mood.

FELICIA: Not because you're a coward?

DON JUAN: Look, I'm sorry if your cheek still stings from the weight of my hand.

FELICIA: Get away from me.

DON JUAN: I just wanted to reason with you.

FELICIA: And you thought brutality was the only way?

DON JUAN: Felicia, come on. It's Don Juan. How long have we known each other?

FELICIA: Too long.

DON JUAN: Hold your tongue, dear.

FELICIA: Truth hurts?

DON JUAN: Let's be reasonable with each other.

FELICIA: I've had years and years of your lousy reasons.

DON JUAN: Then what's another more?

FELICIA: Sonofabitch.

DON JUAN: Think what you say or you'll regret it.

FELICIA: I don't have to think of anything!

[She lunges for Don Juan. They fight. And it is quite a fight! Years and years of pent-up everything (rage, passion, etc.) goes into it. After a while, Marcia enters, interrupting…]

MARCIA: What in God's name is going on here?
FELICIA: I have been insulted and must take revenge.
MARCIA: What revenge? Stop this instant.
FELICIA: Steer clear, Marcia, I'm in no mood for your peace-making. I beg you, out of love for our friendship.
MARCIA: Our friendship? You must think I'm blind.

[Lysander enters]

LYSANDER: Marcia, calm down, hear me out.
MARCIA: Hear you out? Why should I do such a thing? Tell me. Or is it that everyone around here thinks I'm a damn fool?

[Gerry enters, out of breath.]

GERRY: Is everything all right, my dear?
MARCIA: Everything's fine, Gerry. Sit down. And as for you, Lysander, why are you here, anyway?
LYSANDER: Sorry?
MARCIA: Were you perhaps looking for Felicia?
LYSANDER: I don't understand.
MARCIA: Felicia. Felicia.
FELICIA: Remember me?
LYSANDER: I have no reason to look out Felicia.

MARCIA & FELICIA: Really?

LYSANDER: I swear. On my life. My heart's with Marcia.

[Laura enters.]

LAURA: Your heart is with whomever I choose.

LYSANDER: Dear God. Is this a vision? L?

LAURA: Don't start praying now. It doesn't suit you.

LYSANDER: I thought you were in a convent.

LAURA: I haven't been near a convent in years.

LYSANDER: What?

LAURA: Don't get upset. Your eyes get all red and it's not becoming at all.

LYSANDER: I don't understand. What's happening?

LAURA: What's happening is that you have been talking to me night after night.

LYSANDER: No, no, I was talking to Marcia.

LAURA: No, no, you were talking to me.

LYSANDER: You mean -?

LAURA: I was pretending to be Marcia.

LYSANDER: And you -?

MARCIA: Allowed it. Yes. I'd do anything for a friend. I'm a good assistant.

LYSANDER: You tricked me.

LAURA: You did the same.

LYSANDER: This isn't fair!

LAURA: Oh, don't cry those crocodile tears now. No one's going to believe you. *(reveals letter)* Isn't this your signature, Lysander?

LYSANDER: No.

LAURA: You deny you wrote this letter swearing your love? Swearing you'd be my husband?
LYSANDER: I didn't write anything.
LAURA: Who can verify this signature?

[Leon enters]

LEON: I can.
LYSANDER: What are you doing here?
LEON: Joining in the fun.
LAURA: Is this his?
LEON: That's his signature all right. I should know. I've been working for him for a good long while now. Signs my paycheck every week.
LYSANDER: I thought it was every other week.
LEON: No, no, it's every week.
LYSANDER: Since when?
LEON: Since always.
LYSANDER: I never agreed to that.
LEON: I have it in writing.
LYSANDER: Whose writing? What is going on here?
MARCIA: Nothing's going on, except your life. Lysander, it's impossible to avoid what heaven ordains. Laura's yours. Take her hand, and revel in the love of a good woman.
FELICIA: Lysander, don't...
MARCIA: Don't you dare, Felicia. As much as I love you, my hatred for you has grown exponentially over these last few days.
FELICIA: What?
MARCIA: I know all about your act of...treason.

FELICIA: I didn't mean anything –
MARCIA: Enough. Please. Or I'll get upset. And I
don't want to, because it's my wedding day!
LYSANDER & FELICIA: What?
MARCIA: Gerry, take my hand.
GERRY: You're everything to me.
MARCIA: I don't deserve your love, but I'll take it.
And in time, I hope you'll forgive me for how cold I
was to you all these years.
GERRY: There is more forgiveness in my heart than
you know, dear Marcia.
MARCIA: You're a good man, Gerry, and I'm lucky
to have you.

[Marcia and Gerry exit.]

LYSANDER: And I'm lucky to have you.
LAURA: Yes, you are. More than lucky. Downright
fortunate is what you are. After all you've put me
through.
LYSANDER: I'm sorry, Laura, I –
LAURA: Lost your head? Couldn't change your
ways? Just can't help yourself?
LYSANDER: That's not what I mean.
LAURA: I want a proper apology or I swear: you will
never see me again.
LYSANDER: Laura.
LAURA: Swear.
LYSANDER: Laura, I... I'm a jerk, okay? I do the
wrong things, I say the wrong things, I behave badly
and cause people, you, a whole lotta grief. I admit it.

Okay? I'm a louse, I'm every name in the book, but know this: I can change. I will change. I will everything in my power to...

LAURA: Please, don't say another word or you'll ruin it all.

[Felix enters.]

FELIX: Laura, dear Laura, if I may....

LAURA: Dear Felix, there's nothing more to say. I'm yours.

LYSANDER: What?

LAURA: You think just because you swore it in writing you'd win me back? Oh, Lysander, after all you've done, you think I would ever come back to you?

LYSANDER: You can't do this to me. That letter is a legal document.

LAURA: Sue me. Come on, Felix.

FELIX: Are you sure?

LAURA: More than anything.

LYSANDER: I have a right!

LAURA: To what? Screw someone else over? I'm done with you, Lysander.

LYSANDER: But you, but you...

LAURA: Played a good game. That's all.

LYSANDER: Heartless bitch.

LAURA: Heartless is he who abuses love's design. Pay someone with misery, they'll pay you in kind. Remember that. Let's go, Felix. Let's leave this mess.

FELIX: I'll take good care of you. I promise.

LAURA: You've been so good to me already. It'll take years for me to return all the good you've done.

[Felix and Laura exit.]

LEON: Hey. How bout we get out of here and grab ourselves a drink?
LYSANDER: Ten drinks. At least.
LEON: As many as you wish. By the way, did I tell you about this magic potion I got? Well, let me tell you, what you need is a spider's heart…
LYSANDER: A spider?
LEON: Oh. Yeah. And you have to pluck it during a crescent moon…
LYSANDER: What?

[Lysander and Leon exit.]

DON JUAN: Well, that was quite a little show. All's fair in love and war, as the saying goes. (starts to walk away)
FELICIA: Not so quick.
DON JUAN: Will you point your dagger at me forever, Felicia? If you kill me, you kill yourself, for we are one and the same.
FELICIA: We're not.
DON JUAN: More than you think. Light of my soul…
FELICIA: I'll draw blood.
DON JUAN: If it will make you feel better, go ahead. Do it. What will it be, then, Felicia? You or I?
FELICIA: …Neither.

[She withdraws the dagger.]

DON JUAN: I knew you couldn't kill me.
FELICIA: No, but I can do this.

[She slaps him.]

DON JUAN: Getting even, eh?
FELICIA: I haven't even started.

[She kisses him violently.]

After all, what's a little betrayal among friends?

END OF PLAY

THE LABYRINTH OF DESIRE

by Caridad Svich

adapted and translated
from Lope de Vega's *La Prueba de los Ingenios*

Script History:

This text was originally commissioned by and produced at UCSD Dept of Theatre & Dance under Gerardo Ruiz's direction, and developed at New Dramatists in New York City under Jean Randich's direction with cast: Florencia Lozano, Michael Tisdale, Jeffrey Carlson, Andres Munar, Eunice Wong, Simon Kendall, Polly Lee, Carlos Valencia, and Mia Katigbak. It received its professional premiere at Miracle Theatre in Portland, Oregon under Devon Allen's direction. It was subsequently revised, and received production at Moxie Theatre in collaboration with San Diego State University Dept of Theatre & Film in 2010.

Special thanks to Leo Cabranes-Grant, Jorge Huerta, Ursula Meyer, Chris Parry, Gregary Racz, Darko Tresnjak, Phyllis Zatlin and all the actors and designers who have been part of this play's development.

This play is dedicated to the memory of Chris Parry.

A Writer's Labyrinth by Caridad Svich

"To enter that rhythm where the self is lost,
Where breathing: heartbeat: and the subtle music
Of their relation make our dance, and hasten
Us to the moment when all things become
Magic, another possibility."
--Muriel Rukeyser (1962)

The Labyrinth of Desire is a play about transformation and the motor of human desire. Originally written by Lope de Vega in the 1600s under the title *La Prueba de Los Ingenios* (literally "A Test of Wits"), it falls under the category of a *capa y espada*/cloak and dagger play. It is a piece that true to its genre revels in the comedy of love and intrigue, and does so with Lope de Vega's characteristic warmth, wit and poetry. What rises this play above its genre is its great understanding of the essential mutability and fluidity of human desire. Pre-queer theory, pre-feminism and pre-*Sex in the City*, this play challenges the boundaries of prescribed sexual roles, and advocates for the delightful and essential mystery of love. The performance of self, gender identity and sexual identity is at the core of this comedy, yet it also manages to address issues of class and the heteroglossic play of language.

In freely adapting this play for the American stage (and this is the first American English adaptation of this piece), I have taken many liberties with the original text: cutting minor scenes and characters, reassigning some roles and lines, borrowing a very short comedic sequence from Shakespeare's *Troilus and Cressida*, re-shaping and expanding scenes, and adding text of my own to clarify and deepen emotional moments as well as comedic ones. The ending in particular has a new twist that speaks to what I feel were Lope's wholistic intentions with this play. In the use of language I have emphasized the colloquial and direct over the baroque. This choice is actually a mirror of the original's taut and sharp energy. However, the meter and rhythms have necessarily changed. Nevertheless, my intention throughout my conversation with Lope de Vega across the centuries has always been to illuminate his vision for a new audience, one that most likely only knows, if at all, his classic historical play *Fuenteovejuna.* It is an audience, though, that is perhaps familiar with Marivaux's *The Triumph of Love* and surely with Shakespeare's *Twelfth Night* – plays that are clear cousins to this one in spirit, if not in form, and I've taken this into account when re-considering this play. Obviously, this is a free adaptation. It is faithful to Lope's architecture, but it is very much suffused with my own artistic sensibility as a playwright, which also centers on the crossing of normative social and sexual boundaries, women in society, the carnival-esque play with language and genre, and interculturalism. In addition, my history (in my parallel career) as a translator of Federico Garcia Lorca's work, and other dramatists including Calderon de la Barca, has inevitably played a role in my approach to Lope de Vega. Any writer meets a text through their own experience with the page and with the dramatic form. So, call this a hybrid text, a fusion, if you will, of Lope de Vega and Svich. The process has been not unlike the lead character of Florela in this play: I have entered, as Muriel Rukeyser expresses in her poem so eloquently, "the rhythm where the self is lost," and in so doing, have found an exultant vision of transformation.

Figures:

FLORELA, spirited, impulsive, intelligent young woman, 20s

RICARDO, steadfast friend to Florela and Alejandro, 20s

ALEJANDRO, Florela's impetuous, somewhat neurotic, handsome fiancé, 20s

CAMACHO, a young man of quicksilver energy, a messenger, fool, and trickster, 20s

LAURA, confident, poised, intelligent young woman of slightly giddy, neurasthenic energy, 20s

FINEA, her plain-spoken confidante, 20s

PARIS, Laura's charming, ardent suitor, a dandy in the Wilde-an sense with rock star energy, 20s

ESTACIO, his loyal assistant, 20s

DUCHESS (of Ferrara), Laura's mother, sly and elegant, a gracious politician, 40-50s

Setting:

A world of mirrors and transformation.
Simple, elegant and somewhat ornate in design.
A playing area that is open, but can suddenly become
obscured. There is the possibility of magic here and of
getting lost.

Notes:

While anchored in a classical world, the approach to
playing should be fresh, immediate, bold and
contemporary. This play is in the now.

Interval may be taken after Act Two.

Act One

Scene 1

Enter Florela and Ricardo.

Florela: I'll kill myself.
Ricardo: Be reasonable.
Florela: What use has reason in love?
Love has no reason.
Give me your knife.
Ricardo: What?
Florela: So I can plunge it straight into my heart.
Ricardo: Forget him, Florela.
Florela: That's not possible, Ricardo.
Ricardo: Why not?
Florela: Because he…took advantage of me…he lied
to me.
Ricardo: Alejandro's hardly the first man to lie in
love.
Florela: Nor will he be the last,
Is that what you mean?
Ricardo: I only mean –
Florela: He swore he'd marry me, Ricardo. And now
he wants to marry her.
Ricardo: It's outrageous. I know.
Florela: It's shameful. That's what it is.
I give him my body and soul, and he gives me… lies.
Ricardo: Men tend to break their promises
once they have satisfied their desires.
Florela: Are you defending him now?

Ricardo: I speak true. That's all.
Would you rather I lie to you?
Florela: I'd rather there was a way I could stop him
from pursuing her.
Ricardo: If his desire for marriage
Were only driven by love,
I'm sure we could find a way to stop him,
But there is the matter of his
Coming into quite a bit of money
if he does manage to marry Laura.
Her poor mother is desperate to marry her off
before she dies;
If not, she'll lose her inheritance.
Florela: Do you mean to say-?
Ricardo: Alejandro will go to Ferrara
To seek his fortune,
As well as a wife.
Florela: And a pretty wife too, am I right?
Ricardo: Rumor has it.
Florela: Rumor has it she's witty too, is that true?
Ricardo: I'm afraid to say… Laura is Ferrara's shining
star.
Florela: But is she…smart?
Ricardo: She's not your equal;
In matters of learning,
But she holds her own well enough.
Florela: I'd like to see her.
Ricardo: What for?
Florela: I'd like to meet a beautiful and intelligent
woman like her.

Ricardo: Whatever it is you're thinking of doing, it won't end well.

Florela: I'm not thinking of anything.
I'm just afraid she'll fall in love with him, that's all;
Alejandro can be very charming.

Ricardo: He's not the only one who's courting her.
She may not end up with him in the end.

Florela: Let's leave this now;
We'll speak no more about it.
All I ask is that you help me.

Ricardo: To do what?

Florela: Will you help me, Ricardo?

Ricardo: Of course. As long as you stay here.

Florela: I can't.
If Alejandro is going off to
Seek his fortune in Ferrara;
I've no choice but to follow.

Ricardo: Fall out of love, Florela.
You are an intelligent woman,
With a blazing gift for poetry
Astronomy and philosophy.
You've outshone the brightest of scholars,
haven't you?
Well, then, temper love's fury.
Find solace in your own talents,
Your own gifts,
Your own radiant beauty.

Florela: What is it all good for?
What has all the learning in the world
made me fit for?
Love's riddles cannot be solved with books.

I can't stop loving him (as the song goes).[1]
And after what he's done to me,
I won't just stand by and watch while
He marries another.
Ricardo: And if he finds you in Ferrara?
Florela: Let him find me. I'm not afraid of him.
I fear nothing, not even death.
Ricardo: Think of what people will say!
Florela: Let them say what they like.
Ricardo: You'll be the stuff of rumor and gossip.
Florela: They can cackle all they want about me,
The loose tongues and the scolding eyes
With their noses pinched in disapproval.
Let them be heard for miles. They can't destroy me
Nothing they can say will destroy me.
But to lose him –
Yes, that would…
I must stop that marriage.
Ricardo: What will I- ?
Florela: Tell them I had to go to Loreto.
On a spiritual quest.
Ricardo: I will keep your secret. I promise.
Florela: You're a good friend, Ricardo.
Ricardo: (What good it does me).
Florela: Will you check to see if he's gone yet?

---

[1] The song "I Can't Stop Loving You" was a hit for Ray Charles and other singers. Throughout the text there are references to other pop songs that inform the world and emotional register of this piece.

Ricardo: Right away. …Heaven help you.
Florela: I'll need all the help I can get.
Ricardo: Just keep your wits about you;
You'll do fine.

Ricardo walks away.

Florela: Fine, he says.
May his gracious heart be true,
For I am headlong in pursuit.

Exits.

Scene 2

Alejandro enters, followed by Ricardo.

Alejandro: She can chase me all over town
If she likes,
as long as she doesn't
Follow me to Ferrara.
Ricardo: I think that wherever you go,
She's bound to follow.
Alejandro: Why's that?
Ricardo: She's a woman in love.
Alejandro: Meaning?
Ricardo: Love sharpens one's senses.
Hers have always been sharp.
You see what I mean?
Alejandro: Well, she's not to follow me another step
Do you understand?

Ricardo: You're out of love, then?
Alejandro: It's not that I don't love Florela.
I love her as I love myself.
Circumstance is to blame. That's all.
How was I to know I'd be faced
with having to choose
Between two very different women?
One of them, my equal in most things,
Except class, which is a drawback, I admit,
Though I suppose I could live with it;
But what really gets me about Florela
Is that she is too clever by half –
Really, she makes me feel quite stupid sometimes.
I don't cherish feeling like a dim-witted fool
Next to her shining brilliance,
As much as I admire it.
(And there is much to admire in Florela. I admit that).
On the other hand there's Laura:
Who is not only modest and charming,
But graced with a radiant, classical beauty.
Do you see my dilemma?
Ricardo: Well, I…
Alejandro: It's as clear as day,
Especially when you consider
That whoever marries Laura
Will come into quite a fortune.
Ricardo: But such considerations
are not part of love's design.
You should let your passions hold sway
And not merely your ambition.

Alejandro: I owe it to myself
to seek what is best for me.
Florela can cry all she wants to (as the song goes).[2]
I'm off to Ferrara.
Nothing, not even her tears, can stop me.

Sounds offstage.

Camacho: *(Off)* A message from Ferrara, sir!
Alejandro: We've been waiting for you. Come in!
Camacho: *(enters on bicycle)* I can see your Excellency
Was expecting a more distinguished emissary
from the court;
Well, I'm afraid you'll have to make do
With this sweaty mass of aching bones before you.
Camacho's the name, if you must know.
Plain ol' Camacho.
Don't think you would have known my family.
Not your type.
But we're all the same in the end, eh?
When to dust we are turned,
it doesn't matter what family we came from.
We're dust all the same. Isn't that right?
Not that I am reaching the end of my days just yet…
Figure of speech, you understand, turn of phrase.
I sure am thirsty.
You wouldn't be able to spare a drink for a kindly
messenger?

---

[2] The song "It's My Party (and I'll cry if I want to)" was a US pop hit for Lesley Gore.

I was in such a hurry to find this wretched place
I haven't had a drop. That's the truth.
I haven't had a bit of rest.
Alejandro: You'll have plenty of time to rest after I'm
gone.
Camacho: Oh, you're feeling poorly?
Alejandro: What?
Camacho: I'd hate to think you're reaching the end of
your days.
Alejandro: What are you talking about?
Camacho: You said…
Alejandro: I haven't said a thing.
Have I said anything, Ricardo?
Ricardo: Not exactly.
Camacho: My mistake, then.
Alejandro: Yes. Quite.
Camacho: It's good to know you're all right. Good to
know you're in your prime.
Alejandro: Yes. The letter, Camacho.
Camacho: What's that?
Alejandro: May I have the letter?
Camacho: You can have whatever you want
As long as you let me rest.
I tell you, I have pushed myself to the limit,
Do you understand? To the max, as they say.
By the way, I will need a new pair of shoes.
These are absolutely wrecked.
I tore them, you see, on my way here,
So technically they're your responsibility;
Well, not technically
But in actuality, actually.

Good pair of shoes, too. Really liked them.
Had them for years. Trusty pair.
And now? Wrecked. You see my dilemma?
It isn't right. A man needs his shoes.
They mark your place in the world.
What's a man without shoes?
A man without a sole. That's the truth.
Sorry state for any man.
Pitiable, sorry state, if you must know.
Christ, my ass hurts!
No polite way to say it, I'm afraid
(And what does politeness get us anyway?
Smiles and hypocrisy. Not much else that I know.)
I broke my ass riding that shitty bicycle.
Being a messenger isn't what it used to be,
that's for sure.
In the old days… so I've heard…
Messengers had luck on their side,
And plenty of comforts.
What comforts do I have?
Thirst, hunger and a broken ass.
Alejandro *(reading letter)*: I can't believe this.
Camacho: Believe every bit of it.
Nothing but the truth in that letter.
(Oh, I gave it a look a bit earlier.
Had to do something on the road.)
Everyone is after our dear Laura.
No surprise, really.
She's a beautiful woman.
And her mother, the duchess,
could meet her Maker any second.

I wouldn't give her more than a few days myself
I don't mean to be indiscreet;
I'm just telling it how I see it.
No harm intended, if you know what I mean.
There are plenty of men interested in Laura.
I can't think of a man who isn't.
Men of wealth and prestige, too.
Laura has her pick. That's the truth.
She's in a quite a position.
Why, if I wasn't so tired,
So damn hungry, and thirsty and wrecked
By my travels,
I could tell you about all the different kinds of men
That are after our dear Laura
(and she is dear. Oh how dear she is.
If I wasn't who I am;
In my station, as you see,
I, too, would pursue Laura. Make no mistake.)
But such as it is, I can only tell you about…
Well now, I've forgotten.
See? I'm so exhausted I can't even tell things straight.
That's the burden of the job I'm in.
Lapses of memory.
One day I won't remember anything.
…No, wait, there is someone.
Alejandro: Yes?
Camacho: Yes. Yes. Someone indeed. Marseilles.
Alejandro: Who?
Camacho: Paris.
Alejandro: Well, which is it?
Camacho: Huh?

Alejandro: Is it Paris or Marseilles?

Camacho: Paris, of course. What kind of stupid name is Marseilles?

Alejandro: You said…

Camacho: I did not say Marseilles.

You must be hearing things, sir.

It's not a good sign to hear things.

Once the senses start to go, well…

No polite way to say it, but it's straight to the crapper.

Alejandro: What?

Camacho: Shit hole in the earth, bone-yard, grave, you get my meaning?

Best watch yourself, or you won't even get to Ferrara

To meet our beautiful Laura.

Not at this rate.

Alejandro: I'm fine, Camacho.

Camacho: Glad to hear it.

Young, handsome devil like you:

It'd be shame if you were out of circulation.

Alejandro: So, his name…this suitor…

Camacho: Yes. Paris. I'm sure you've heard of him.

He's a very smart fellow.

Always has the latest fashion on. Well-groomed too.

He's a real hit with the ladies.

And after Paris, there's Leonardo the Frenchman,

Balduino the Italian, Octavio, Lisandro, and….

Alejandro: That's enough. You're depressing me.

Camacho: I'm just telling the truth.

Alejandro: Yes, well…some truths are…

Not worth hearing.

I'll go to Ferrara,

And when I arrive, those who fawn over Paris
Might just find themselves fawning over me.
I'm worth it, after all.
Camacho: You've cash on you?
Alejandro: Of course.
Camacho: Then you'll be fine.
It always takes a bit of cash
To get people on your side.
Alejandro: Clever fellow, aren't you?
Where are you from?
Camacho: Spain, sir.
A sus ordenes, se~nor.
Just a lowly messenger. That's me.
I work for old Clarindo.
He hired me after I left University.
I earned my bachelor's degree,
But what good does it do me?
Everybody's gone to University these days.
The world is populated with graduates
Who don't have a pot to piss in.
Sorry to be blunt, but that's the truth, sir.
Nothing but fancy degrees in our pockets,
And no proper jobs to speak of.
Alejandro: Would you like to work for me?
Camacho: Ol' Clarindo wouldn't mind
watching me go.
That's the truth. He's never had much real use for me.
Alejandro: Then, it's settled. Let's go.
Camacho: About my salary…
Alejandro: Don't worry.
There will be plenty of perks.

Camacho: Heaven knows I could use some perks.
I haven't had a perk in a good long while,
If you know what I mean?
Yes, sir. It's a miracle.
Alejandro: What?
Camacho: My aches.
I don't know what it is,
But they're cured all of sudden.
Wonder of the world, eh?
Alejandro: Ricardo?
Ricardo: Yes?
Alejandro: If Florela comes looking for me,
Tell her that wherever Laura is,
that's where she can find me.

Exit Alejandro and Camacho in one direction, Ricardo in another.

Scene 3

Enter Laura and Finea.

Laura: I'm not going to find anyone who can please me.
Finea: I don't see why not.
Laura: I do. I see it all too well, Finea. I just can't put it into words.
Finea: I've never known you to be shy.
Laura: I'm not,
But there are too many men, Finea.
So many men…

To have all these men chasing after me
just makes me want to be alone.
Besides, I've never taken to men
Whose interest in me
had more to do with my mother's wealth
Than with my honest love.
Finea: What do you expect?
You're never going to find
Someone who's truly worthy of you.
Such a man doesn't exist.
It's best if you concentrate
On who you really want.
Let desire guide you.
You'll have more fun that way.
Anyway, being rich
Isn't such a bad thing,
(what I wouldn't give….)
So, who is it that gets your heart racing?
Is it Paris? Is it? Come on. Admit it. He's a looker.
Laura: He's handsome. Yes.
Finea: Rumor has it he's your favorite.
Laura: Rumor has it wrong. I don't have a favorite.
Every time I see someone whom I think
"Well, maybe, he's the one,"
I can see their eyes
Sparkling with lust
For my mother's estate.
Finea: You want romance, eh?
You're such a softie.
Laura: I'm not.
Finea: You're tenderhearted.

Laura: I'm not excessively tenderhearted.
Finea: You can't stand the idea of marriage
As a simple business transaction,
Which is what it is, after all.
No. You'd rather be wooed and won.
Laura: What of it?
I'll not give any man my heart
Until he shows me he deserves it.
I need to be loved for who I am
And nothing more.
My happiness depends upon it.

Florela appears, somewhat disguised.

Florela: *(aside)* Your happiness and mine.
Dear lady, you don't know me
But I've traveled far
to get a mere glimpse of your beauty,
and be able to delight,
in your wit.
I hope you will see fit
To allow me the honor of your presence,
If only for a moment.
Laura: A moment and more
If you continue to please me with such exquisite
words.
Florela: I'll do my best to please you.
Would you give me your hand?
Laura: Only my hand?
Were I the sun,
I would give you my rays,

For I could never compete
With the light that shines
So gently from your eyes.
Florela: Please, don't say such things,
For it is I who am humbled by your radiant beauty.
I beg you: please, don't look at me,
For if you do, I'll have to look away,
Or else let myself be blinded by your splendor.
Everything I've heard is true:
You're nothing short of a miracle.
Laura: Such kind words from such a kind person…
Florela: You must be wondering who I am.
Laura: I can't say I'm not curious,
For that would be a lie,
And I do not care for lies.
Florela: Nor do I.
Laura: We're in agreement.
Florela: Yes.
Laura: Good. I like that we think alike.
Tell me everything about you.
Florela: There's nothing much to tell.
I was on my way to Loreto
When I came upon your door.
I'd heard so much about you,
I couldn't go on without seeing you
With my own eyes.
My story is small,
And insignificant in the world's grand design.
But there it is:
I'm merely a woman,
Loyal and true,

Who would like to serve you,
If you'll let me.
You see, I am noble of heart, but not of blood.
Laura: And your name…?
Florela: Diana.
Laura: The huntress.
Florela: Only your humble servant. Nothing more.
Laura: And you're not otherwise engaged?
Florela: If I were, would I offer myself so freely?
Laura: I thought you were on your way to Loreto.
Florela: I was. I am. But…things change.
Laura: As the moon changes?
Florela: You'll find me true. I promise you.
My changeable being is only reflected in my name:
Diana.
Everything else about me is fixed,
And anchored to you.
Laura: I am your ship, then?
Florela: If you like.
Laura: Stay with me.
If you do,
I'll offer you all that I have:
my very self.
Florela: I don't know how to thank you.
I came here in hope that I could serve you,
But to have my hope become a reality
Is a true blessing.
I promise I'll do my very best.
Laura: I've no doubt.
Florela: Indeed, I think you'll find me more than
capable. For I've gifts that -

Laura: Your cleverness will
make you a most valued friend.
Florela: I could also be your secretary, if you wish.
I am fluent in several languages,
and my wit is known to be quite keen.
Laura: Your talents are clear.
In fact, I'd like you to help me.
I don't know if you're aware, but
I'm facing quite a difficult decision
in my life right now,
I need the guidance of someone I can trust,
someone who is impartial to my circumstances,
and who can be absolutely discreet.
Do you understand?
Florela: Yes.
Laura: You see, my mother is obsessed
with marrying me off before she dies.
She means well. Make no mistake,
She's had men come here from all over
And letters arrive every day as well.
Florela: Letters?
Laura: Oh. You know. Love letters.
Florela: Really?
Laura: Oh. Yes. Hundreds of them.
Florela: For you?
Laura: Of course. Who else?
Florela: Naturally.
Laura: They're sweet, most of them.
You know, the usual stuff:
"I can't wait to meet you, I dream about you…"
on and on and on.

But some, well,
- How can I put it? -
some write rather shocking and inappropriate things.
Not my style, really.
So, I'm not sure how to reply.
I mean, I should reply, right?
Florela: Well…it depends on the letter…
Laura: I just need someone I can count on. You see?
You're deft.
Florela: What?
Laura: And cunning.
Florela: Well, I…
Laura: You must guide me, Diana;
you must guide me, like a star,
Through this labyrinth,
So I can make the decision of my life.
Florela: It'd be an honor to do
whatever I can to guide you.
I've heard of your dilemma.
I even know some of the men involved;
Know *of* them, I should say.
Their reputation precedes them.
Of course, you'll need help
replying to letters and the like.
I'll be happy to handle your correspondence.
Whatever you need, you can count on my discretion.
Laura: I trust you won't be shy about giving me
Your advice as I consider my options.
Florela: Not at all. I'm nothing, if not forthright.
Laura: And we'll talk for hours and hours, yes?

Florela: Whatever you wish.

Laura: It'll be good to talk

And distract ourselves

from sorting through all these suitors,

all these men…:

They're such a bore.

Florela: That's because none of them

are worthy of you.

There will be one who is, though. I'm sure of it.

Finea: Oh, would you just look at them?

They're so delicious.

Laura: What are you going on about?

Finea: The men, Florela. The men.

They're all out on the terrace! See?

[The suitors – Paris with Estacio, Ricardo as Infante,
Alejandro with Camacho, etc. - can be seen as if on a
fashion runway. All strut and pose. A blast of David
Bowie's "All the Young Dudes" or the like plays. And then
they exit…]

Laura: What do you think, Diana?

Florela: Well, I…

Laura: It's your choice.

I'll have whomever you think is worthy.

Florela: It'd help me if you could tell me

What you were looking for.

Laura: You know what I want. You know me.

Florela: Well, not really…

Laura: Yes, you do.

Your wishes are my wishes. Don't you see?

Dear Diana, from now on my life will revolve
Around our friendship and love.
Florela: Then, as Diana, I am moon to your sun.
Whatsoever shines in me is merely a reflection
 of your beauty and constancy.
Laura: And whatsoever shines in you
Is testament to my happiness,
For you have restored my faith in life again.

Laura and Finea walk away; Florela stays behind for a moment.

Florela: *(aside)* Oh Alejandro,
The moon will come crashing upon the earth
Before you ever marry Laura.

Scene 4

Enter Paris (the Duchess of Urbino's son), followed by his assistant Estacio.

Paris: Estacio?
Estacio: What is it, sir?
Paris: Has Alejandro arrived yet?
Estacio: Alejandro, Alejandro…
Paris: Alejandro. You know.
Estacio: Oh. Alejandro. Yes. He certainly has arrived.
Paris: And?
Estacio: Well, Paris, what can I say?
Paris: Say.
Estacio: I've never seen a man

who cuts such an imposing figure.
Everybody's swooning over him, and rightly so.
Paris: Swooning how?
Estacio: You know, arms and legs like so…
eyes cast to the heavens.
Intense kind of swoon. The kind reserved for gods.
Paris: What? Is he -?
Estacio: He's young, handsome, dark;
Paris: What else?
Estacio: Long legs. Like a horse.
Strong, lean, pure muscle.
He's ripped. You can tell.
Even with his clothes on.
Paris: What kind of clothes?
Estacio: The best of the best, the latest fashion.
Soft silk, luscious linen.
In the most exquisite hues of royal blue.
Paris: Well, so what?
He's rich. I'm rich too. That makes us equal.
Estacio: Not quite.
Paris: What do you mean?
Laura's not the kind of woman
Who is easily impressed by signs of wealth.
She'll choose whomever she likes,
If she ever gets around to it.
I'm a bit worried about his size, though.
Estacio: There is that.
Paris: You said he's tall?
Estacio: That, too.
But he's not the only one
you need to keep an eye out for.

There's a man known as the Infante of Aragon.
He's a fearless sonofabitch.
Has taken on thousands of men in battle.
Paris: Thousands?
Estacio: So they say.
Paris: And is he courting Laura now too?
Estacio: So it seems.
Paris: This is impossible!
How am I supposed to make
any kind of impression on Laura,
If she's... if every man...
What is this sonofabitch like?
Estacio: The Infante?
Paris: Yes, yes, the Infante. How did he arrive?
Estacio: On a black stallion, no less. Like a true warrior.
Paris: I wish I'd thought of making an entrance like that.
Estacio: Come.
We can see them better from over here.[3]
I'll call out their names as they pass by.
Just remember to keep an eye out for Alejandro.

[Infante appears on terrace, a pose and wave to the paparazzi and the admiring crowd.]

That's
The Infante: isn't he something?

---

[3] This viewing sequence is adapted from Shakespeare's *Troilus and Cressida.*

O brave Infante!
Isn't he brave?
Paris: Yes, yes: a brave man.
Estacio: And gallant, too, so I've heard.
Gallant and brave.
I wonder where... There he is!

[Alejandro appears also on the terrace, a paparazzi moment.]

Paris: Who?
Estacio: Alejandro.
Paris: Calm down, will you?
Estacio: Just look at him.
O admirable
youth! Not a day past twenty-three.
Go your way, Alejandro, go

[Infante and Alejandro walk away.]

your way! Had I a sister or
a daughter, he could do what he will....
Paris: That's enough. My envy is sufficiently aroused.
Estacio: The Duchess is coming.
Paris: Who do you think Laura will choose?
Estacio: Whoever's the least deserving.

Enter the Duchess of Ferrara.

Duchess: The more suitors that continue to arrive
the more worried and confused I become.

Paris: I kiss your feet.[4]

Duchess: Oh, Paris, it's you!

Paris: Are you all right, ma'am?

Duchess: Given the state I'm in,
How could I possibly be all right?
I'm overcome with sadness.
As the great philosopher once said
"It's not merely illness, but rather melancholy
That will surely send a woman to an early grave."

Paris: May I enquire as to the source of your sadness,
ma'am?

Duchess: You may.

Paris: You're most kind. Always, so very kind.

Duchess: The source of my sadness, good man,
Is that I am inundated with men.

Paris: I'm sorry?

Duchess: Men who have come to seek my dear
Laura's hand.

Paris: You should be happy, ma'am.

Duchess: Happy?

Paris: Surely it should be a comfort to you
That Laura has so many deserving men
to choose from,
So many who desire her hand.
If anything, you should be flattered,
(If I may say so).
Out of so many men,

_____

[4] In the source text, Lope de Vega satirizes courtly manners and conventions. In this version, the emphasis is on the erotic fetish, even the promise of a touch, reflecting the omnisexual energies radiating throughout the piece.

you are bound to find someone truly worthy
Of your daughter.
Duchess: Paris, I don't want to die
Knowing I've engendered
the ill-will of all the friends that I have made
during my life.
Once Laura chooses,
And she will choose by herself, for herself,
All the parents of those men
Will come to me and ask me for an explanation.
They'll be hurt. Do you understand?
Because they won't understand
That I didn't have
Or won't have
anything to do with Laura's decision.
Paris: But what if you don't approve?
Duchess: It's up to her, whether I approve or not.
Paris: But her choice might cost you long-standing
friendships and…
Duchess: Where's Laura? Where's my dear girl?
Estacio: Last I saw her she was in the garden
With Diana, her secretary.
They're rarely apart these days.
Duchess: I've never seen such a love.
Estacio: If I may, ma'am?
Duchess: Yes, Estacio?
Estacio: I think Diana is most deserving
Of her lady's favor.
She's a lovely woman, this Diana.
I see them every day
Near the fountains,

Or seated by the statues,
And I can't help but admire how they read and write
And carry on with such pure joy.
What I'd give to have a joy like that...
Duchess: Bring Laura to me.
Estacio: Yes, ma'am.
Duchess: At once.
Estacio: Right away, ma'am. Excuse me.

Estacio Exits.

Duchess: If Laura is devoting herself all day
to poetry and reading, and loving Diana,
it's no wonder she has no desire to marry.
Paris: What's this woman like?
Duchess: Diana? Oh, she's brilliant. No question.
I wasn't won over at first.
I thought "Oh, it's all just talk."
So, I had the country's most
learned scholars over here
and had them engage in a debate with her;
She showed them –
Not only what she knew,
But that she knew
more than all of them put together.
It was amazing.
Paris: I can imagine.

Enter Laura.

Laura: What can I do for you, mother?

Duchess: Ah, my dear Laura, my darling girl.

Laura: Yes, mother.

Duchess: Why do you neglect me so?

Why do you run away from me like a wounded lover,

when you know no one loves you like I do.

Laura: Rest assured, I'm not running away from you,

but rather, the world.

Duchess: But why, dear girl?

You've all these suitors. All these men.

All you have to do is make a choice.

Ease my suffering, child.

Let me have a peaceful death.

Paris: *(aside)* Oh, God!

It's clear that the Duchess wants

To give her away to me.

Laura: Your happiness is my happiness.

Tell me whom I should choose.

Paris: *(aside)* May my name caress her tongue.

Duchess: It is you who must tell me, dear.

I'll consent to whomever you choose.

Laura: I suspect you want me to pick Paris.

Otherwise you wouldn't say all these things

In his presence.

Mom…

Duchess: Speak up. Don't be afraid.

Paris: *(aside)* Oh Lord and all the heavenly stars,

Look here upon this man in love;

Look here upon this man in pain

And ardor;

Have pity on me.

Let her choose me, I pray you.
By all the powers in heaven and earth,
I commend you to let her see what is right:
Please, Lord, make her choose me.
Force her if you have to,
Force the stars in our favor.
Laura: Give me three more days to decide.
Duchess: Three days it is, but after three days
You must end this interminable saga.
Think of the state
all these poor men are in.
Think of the state
your poor mother is in.
Have mercy, dear child.

Exit all, except Laura.

Laura: This is impossible.
I can't rush into this decision.
If I do, I may end up with the wrong person,
And then what?
I'll have no one else to blame
But myself
when my love begins to fall apart.
I don't know what to do.
I'm losing myself.

Scene 5

Enter Florela

Florela: I was beginning to think I'd lost you.

Laura: No. Never.

Florela: Then why are you out here
All alone?
You know I can't stand the thought
Of not being with you.

Laura: I know. I know. I feel the same.
I just can't move, that's all.

Florela: What are you talking about?

Laura: I'm in shock.

Florela: Why? What did your mother say to you?

Laura: Only that she wants to break my heart.

Florela: Don't say such things.
Your mother wants the best for you.

Laura: You warned me. Didn't you?
Time and again,
you warned me this day would come.
Oh, Diana, what am I to do?

Florela: I can't stand to see you like this.
It's worse than not being with you.
What's happened? Tell me.

Laura: She told me that I must decide.
And she did so in the manner
of a dying woman begging the heavens
For peace upon her soul.
It's most upsetting,
As you can imagine,
To think I have made my mother suffer
So very much…
And for what?
For my own happiness?

Florela: It matters.

Laura: Of course it matters.

But I've been selfish in my indecision.

She's been a good mother,

And what do I do?

I tell her I need three more days

To choose,

When the fact of the matter is,

I'd need a lifetime.

Who do you think is best, Diana?

Paris?

The Infante? Alejandro?

…

It's Alejandro, isn't it?

I must admit even before I saw him,

His name was music to my ears.

Alejandro, Alejandro….

What enchantments do you bring?

Sweet enchantments,

Alejandro, to those ardent for your spring.

…

What? Have I said something wrong?

Diana, just because I'm getting married

Doesn't mean I'll forget you.

I could never forget you.

You're my moon, my little huntress.

What we have is a pure and honest love.

…

Don't cry.

If you cry, you'll make me cry too.

You know how I am. I am easily moved.

Come on. Wipe those tears off your face.
Rejoice in my happiness.
Besides, who says we can't be friends
Even after I'm married?
Florela: If only I could tell you, Laura,
if only I could tell you the truth.
Laura: I know no one truer than you.
Florela: Stop. Please. Don't... say such things to me.
Laura: What do you mean? Diana?
Florela: I don't know how I... I can't tell you.
Laura: You can tell me everything.
Florela: If I tell you everything,
You won't ever wish to see me again.
Laura: What are you saying?
Florela: I should kill myself,
As I should've done from the start.
Put an end to all deception.
Laura: Stop. You're frightening me.
Please. Whatever it is, you can tell me.
How can a friendship be true
if it is not based on honesty?
Say what you need to say.
I promise I won't run away from you.
Florela: If only I could dare...
Laura: You secrets are safe with me.
Do not worry.
Even if you divulged
You were part of a plot to kill my mother
I'd guard your secret,
even at the expense of my heart.

Florela: What if somebody comes in?

Laura: We'll throw caution to the wind.

Florela: I don't know if I can say it.

Laura: Say it!

Florela: I am…dear lady,

Whom the heavens admire so,

And the sun gazes upon with sweet envy,

I am…Laura…

a man.

Laura: Oh God!

Florela: You see why I didn't want to tell you.

Laura: You're…a man?

Florela: I can go back to being a woman

If you like.

We can just forget about all this.

However you did say you'd guard my secret

With your life.

Laura: Well, I didn't know then what I was…

Getting myself into…

I really don't know what to say…

This must be some kind of trick,

Some kind of test.

You're so clever, after all.

Florela: It's no trick, Laura.

Just don't ask me for proof.

That would be a dangerous request.

Laura: How can expect me to…?

Look at you.

Your face, your hair, the way you move…

What you say and what I see

Are two different things.

You can't be a man.
Men don't, aren't… Like you.
Florela: Listen to me, Laura.
Laura: No. I don't want to hear another word.
Florela: I must not mean very much to you
If you won't even hear me out.
Laura: What more could you possibly say,
Or is it that you wish to wound me further?
Florela: I wish nothing of the kind, believe me.
Just let me explain…
You can have me killed later.
I'll take my punishment as it comes.
Laura: Diana is a man. Diana is a man.
Impossible!
Florela: But didn't you wish all along
That I was a man?
You must've wished it in secret.
Otherwise you wouldn't be so shocked.
You said you loved me once.
Remember?
We were walking past the fountain
On the far edge of the garden
And you said
"If you were a man, I'd be yours."
Well, here I am.
A miracle of love has occurred.
I've changed my sex for you.
Isn't that enough?
What more do you want?
What more do you want from me?

Laura: Nothing… I'm just…

Florela: Angry?

Laura: No…Afraid.

What if the person I've fallen in love with

Suddenly transforms himself back into a woman

On our wedding night?

Florela: I wouldn't. I couldn't.

I'm a man.

Look, when I was a boy

I accidentally killed a wealthy man,

A nobleman, you see?

It was an accident, pure and simple,

But my parents feared for my life nonetheless,

So they disguised me as a girl.

I had six sisters, and as I grew up,

I became not only familiar with feminine ways

But quite, well, feminine, to most eyes.

In disguise, as I've spent almost my entire life,

When I heard of you

And had occasion to see your beautiful portrait;

And once I did, I fell in love,

And my love led me here –

As you see.

You trusted me so much

I couldn't find a way to tell you

Without fearing I'd break your heart.

The truth is, I can't live without you.

I won't.

If you marry now,

it would kill me.

Laura: … don't cry.
You'll just make me cry too.
I believe you. It's an odd story, but
I want to believe you, so I will.
I can't tell you what I feel for you.
If I did, I'd…
You've betrayed me and my mother's house;
You know that?
And yet, my love for you,
My love for your beauty and intellect
and tenderness….
obliges me to delay your punishment
And possibly even my marriage.
Florela: Give me your feet.
Laura: …No. I can't… I can't be alone with you.
What's your real name?
Florela: Felipe
Laura: Felipe…what a sweet name.
Florela: It's what it is.
Laura: Listen, Felipe,
we only have three days.
What can we do
to get rid of all these men?
There must be something….
Florela: Patience, love.
I need your patience.
I've a scheme that will put off your
wedding for quite some time.
Laura: What is it?
Florela: Rather than choosing to your taste
(and thus potentially angering

so many deserving men
And their families)
You'll have a competition instead:
A test of wits:
The one who can most ingeniously decipher
A series of clever riddles
(devised by me, of course)
Will earn your hand in marriage,
And become your rightful husband.
Laura: That's perfect! Oh, you're so clever, Diana.
Florela: Felipe.
Laura: Shhh! I fear Mother might find us.
I thought I heard her just now.
Florela: Listen.
Laura: What?
Florela: Shall we carry on… as friends?
Laura: I don't know. I can't quite describe it
But I can't look at you in the same way
As I did before.
Florela: I understand;
Let's speak about this later…
In the mean time, we must use our wits
To make our way through this labyrinth of desire.

ACT Two

Scene 6

Ricardo, disguised as the Infante,[5] followed by Estacio. This scene should have the aura of attraction about it. Ricardo as

*the Infante exudes aggressive sexual energy which sparks
Estacio's desire. Think: bull and matador vibe.*

Ricardo: This is absurd.
Why do I, the Infante of Aragon,
Have to put up with some silly riddles
Just to win a woman's heart?
Estacio: She's not just any woman, sir.
Ricardo: No. She's Laura, beautiful Laura,
We know that, but you know what I mean....don't
you know, man?
Estacio: Well, I...
Ricardo: Give me a gun. Let's duel it out.
That's the only way to solve things.
Estacio: Well, there are other ways, sir.
Ricardo: For you, maybe.
I'm a soldier. That's my training.
That's what I'm fit for.
Guns and knives, my friend. Those are the tools of my
trade. I ask you, Estacio, I ask you.
Estacio: Sir?
Ricardo: What is this riddle supposed to mean?
Estacio: Well, I...
Ricardo: It has three sections, no less.
Look at them.
What am I supposed to do with them?

---

[5] Masking and disguise in this text throughout is another way to keep
the imaginative play of desire alive; thus, manifestations of other sides
of the self are brought to the surface, perhaps, aspects of the self which
cannot be released otherwise. It is suggested that in production, the
quality of disguise should be elegant and subtle, and not just handled
for broad comic effect.

Estacio: It's only one riddle, sir.

Ricardo: Would that it were only one riddle.

No. There's to be an oral exam, too.

Estacio: Oral?

Ricardo: Given by none other than her secretary.

Estacio: Diana? Really?

Ricardo: What am I going to do?

I'm no good at exams. I never was.

Not even in school.

Estacio: Don't get upset, sir. That's no way to prepare
yourself.

Ricardo: Listen, I am the Infante of Aragon.

Do you understand?

(I must make him believe me.

Oh Florela, if you only knew what I do for you.)

I, the Infante of Aragon,

will not be belittled by a...secretary,

Even if it is Diana.

Estacio: Well, she is no ordinary secretary.

Ricardo: All I know is thanks to her

A labyrinth is being created in the palace garden

As the final obstacle

in this ridiculous contest.

First, the riddle of the damn Sphinx,

Then, the debate

And then, the labyrinth.

And not only do we have to

find our way through

the damned labyrinth –

No, that would be too easy -

But we have to do so

In total darkness,
Like the Minotaur-
Estacio: You better get yourself a thread.
Ricardo: A thread? A damn compass is what I need!
And if I reach the labyrinth's heart,
If I get there,
Who will be waiting for me?
None other than our dear, ravishing Laura.
Well, you know what I think?
I think why bother going after Laura?
I'll just pursue Diana instead.
Her cleverness is all I need.
Estacio: She's clever all right,
But she also has other qualities
I think you'll appreciate.
Oh look, Alejandro has just come in.
Ricardo: You must tell me all about this Diana…
Estacio: I will, but…
Ricardo: Now, man. No time like the present.
Estacio: It's best if we talk somewhere else.
Ricardo: Discretion, eh? I'm with you there, friend.
When talking about a woman,
It's best to use the utmost discretion.

Exeunt the Infante and Estacio.
Scene 7

Enter Alejandro, followed by Camacho.

Camacho: What are you staring at that piece of paper for? You're going to hypnotize it.

Alejandro: I'm going to memorize it
So that when I die I can say it was a piece of paper
That ruined my chances at a better life.

Camacho: What are you talking about?

Alejandro: Women, Camacho.
What else would I be talking about?
Women are as changeable as the damned moon!

Camacho: Don't give up now, sir. You've just started.

Alejandro: It's that secretary's fault.
If it wasn't for her, Laura would be mine by now.

Camacho: You're getting all bent out of shape, sir,
Over what? It's just a little riddle,
A piffle, a twaddle, if you ask me
(And you're asking, aren't you?
I can see it in your eyes, sir.
You've got the world to ask of me.)
Well, I tell you, I'm up to the test, sir.
This trifling riddle may be a boggle to put together,
But it's a toggled boggle we can solve. Yes, sir.
No question about it. Mark my words.
If I don't solve this waffle,
may I lose my head.

Alejandro: You're a good man, Camacho.

Camacho: I'm a fool, sir, but I've my honor.
That's the truth.
What's a fool without honor
But a wretched, pitiable fool?
I will not be pitied, sir.
I'll be laughed at, but not pitied.

Give me two days. If I haven't solved
The riddle by then,
Well then, you can have your way with me, sir.
Alejandro: You mean that?
Camacho: Off with my head.
Alejandro: Well, I'll be eager to see what you can do.
Camacho: Your faith in me is most heartening.
Now, then, let's take a look at this silly little riddle…
Hmmm… Hmmm…
Alejandro: Have you solved it?
Camacho: Just reading, sir. Taking it in.
The only way to make headway with a riddle
Is to take it in, absorb its intricacies.
Alejandro: …Well?
Camacho: These are rather negligible verses, if you
ask me. They're simply mired in imperfection.
Alejandro: I thought they were rather nice.
Camacho: Nice? You like this, sir?
I am, I am not; I love what I love not;
I delude with disillusion,
I stir envy and confusion;
And it is from envy that I will die,'
(That's sad, isn't it? To die from envy.
That's very sad. Reminds me of my uncle Roblan.
He got caught up in quite a tangle once….)
Alejandro: Go on, Camacho.
Camacho: Sorry. 'In my suffering lies my cure,
in my death lies a dream of life;'
(Dream of life. That's nice.
She's done quite well there.)
'Remember me as one forgotten;

I am content in my discontent,
For I retreat to move ahead;
Soon I will be nothing,
But in my nothingness, I will be more
Than anyone who is truly nothing
that seeks to live upon these shores.'.
(That last bit is rather existentialist.)
Alejandro: What?
Camacho: Nothing.
Just a random thought that entered my brain.
Alejandro: We've no time for random thoughts.
Do you think you can you solve this in two days?
Camacho: I can solve it in less.
Alejandro: You're a genius, Camacho! I love you!
Camacho: No need to get overexcited now.
Alejandro: No, you're right, even if you do solve it,
Camacho: Which I will.
Alejandro: There's still the damned labyrinth to deal
with. How will we ever meet Laura's enchanting gaze
In that ridiculous maze?
Rumor has it
it's so dark and confusing
that a man is bound to lose himself,
and spend the rest of his days
wandering the sinuous alleys and twisted curves
of its cursed construction
until death becomes his only solution.
Camacho: Don't worry about the labyrinth;
when it's done, I'll go see it for myself.
Believe me, I'll find your precious Laura
With no more than

A fine bottle of wine and a cheap lantern.

Alejandro: Haven't you heard a word I've said?
You can't take a lantern, you stupid idiot.
You have to go into the labyrinth in the dark.
That's the damned test!

Camacho: Oh. In the dark.

Alejandro: That's what 'no light' usually means.

Camacho: Well then, that's a different story
altogether. I'll have to give it some thought.

Alejandro: I should kill myself now, and get it over
with.

Camacho: No need to rush things.
This 'no light' business is tricky
But it won't have us tricked.
We'll just have to….
Think of something else.
Correct me if I'm wrong, but this
Riddle-and-labyrinth business
Is all Diana's idea, isn't it?

Alejandro: Yes. So?

Camacho: It's simple, then.

Alejandro: I'm afraid you've lost me.

Camacho: Love, my friend.
Love is what unmoors a person.
Love is what sets someone off course.
Love is what changes someone's destiny.
You follow me?

Alejandro: Love?

Camacho: Yes.
Now, suppose a charming suitor comes along
And offers Diana his hand in marriage?

Think what secrets a woman in love
Is bound to reveal to such a gentle and
Handsome man?

Alejandro: We'll have to find a man, then.

Camacho: Look no further.

Alejandro: The thing is, there aren't any suitable men for miles. It's going to be quite a search.

Camacho: Not really.

Alejandro: I mean, where are we going to find
a handsome, gallant, brave man
Who can compete with,
No, not compete, but match Diana
Thought for thought,
Word for word,
Action for action?
I'm afraid there's no one.
There's not a man around who's worthy of her.
We'd do best to pack our things
and resign ourselves
To our circumstances.
Admit defeat.
That's the only course of action left to us.

Camacho: Not the only…

Alejandro: What are you talking about?

Camacho: A man.

Alejandro: What man? There is no man.

Camacho: Yes, there is.

Alejandro: Who?

Camacho: I'm a man, sir.

Alejandro: You?

Camacho: Last I checked.

Alejandro: What can you do?

Camacho: I can be a proper gentleman.

I'm just a bit out of practice.

Alejandro: A bit?

Camacho: Look, if I pretend to be a nobleman,

I'll be able to court Diana without

Arousing suspicion of any kind.

I'm quite a lover, sir.

Put me in a room with Diana

And not only will she reveal every secret

she has to me, but her very soul, too.

Alejandro: *(aside)* Shall I give this lunatic a chance?

Camacho: What have you to lose, sir,

But your very life?

Alejandro: All right, but we can't just give you

clothes, you'll have to have a house as well.

Camacho: Oh, I don't need a house, sir.

Just give me a footman or two; They should do me.

I can get by with very little, you see.

Alejandro: How' bout a name?

Camacho: Don Lucas de Galicia.

Alejandro: And your title?

Camacho: The Marquis of Mal-Odor.

Alejandro: I hope no one smells a rat.

Camacho: The perfume of angels, my friend.

Nothing but the sweet, delicate perfume

Of life's illusions and life's dreams.

Exit Camacho and Alejandro.

Scene 8

Enter Florela and Laura.

Florela: Give me your hand.
Tell me what you see in me.
I need to know how I seem to you.
Laura: You seem more beautiful than before.
Neither my eyes or ears find cause for sadness.
Florela: If you have any complaint about my hands,
I'd be more than happy to show you what they can
do.
Laura: Hands off! We agreed.
Though I've no doubt your hands can work wonders.
Florela: I have to tell you something.
Laura: Tell me, then. Why make me wait?
Felipe, can't you see that my love
For you grows by the hour?
Florela: Is it possible that one day you could be my
wife? Or am I truly dreaming?
Laura: Marriage diminishes love's pleasure.
Its duty has its cost.
Let's talk about something else. Not love.
Florela: What else could we talk about if not love?
I am suspended in your orbit,
Restless with desire.
Laura: We could talk about a rival.
Florela: A rival? What rival?
Laura: Alejandro, of course.
Florela: …You are cruel and merciless
And undeserving of my love.

Laura: What are you saying?

Florela: How could you possibly think
we could just chatter on about Alejandro
as if it meant nothing?

Laura: I don't understand.

Florela: I offer you my heart,
And you bring jealousy into the room.
You twist my love into knots
And delight in my suffering.
What kind of woman are you?

Laura: Felipe.

Florela: Don't…say my name with those treacherous
lips.

Laura: You're upset.

Florela: Of course I'm upset. How could I not be
upset when you bring up Alejandro just like that?
You might as well throw my heart into the fire.

Laura: Felipe, I'm sorry,
I didn't mean to upset you.
It's just that I trust you
And well, who else am I going to turn to?
We've confided so much in each other.
I don't know what else to do…
What should I do with Alejandro?
He wants to see me on the terrace tonight.
And well, he's been quite persuasive.

Florela: I don't believe this.
You still don't know what to do?
Go on, then. Talk to Alejandro, see Alejandro,
Be with Alejandro.
Leave me out of it. I won't be jealous.

151

It was bound to happen, right?
Alejandro is your equal. Marry him instead;
but don't ask me for my opinion ever again.
I can't be your advisor anymore.
That's a role I won't play.
What I must do now is to try and forget you:
Erase you from my mind as best I can.
I'll kill myself
And with my death
all memory of you will be gone.
If love is in the blood, then in spilling blood
I will rid myself of all the love that is inside me.
Laura: Felipe, look at me. Please.
I can't bear to see you like this.
Look at me, my darling.
Florela: Get off me, Laura. Off!
My tears are mine, and mine alone.
They're not for your pleasure
Or amusement.
Laura: Please stay with me, Felipe.,
Let's start again.
Florela: No. It's over.

Exit Florela.

Laura: Sweet woman, sweet man, come back to me.
I love you both. Don't you see?
You've put a spell on me (as the song goes)[6]

---

[6] "I've Put a Spell on You" was a hit for Screamin Jay Hawkins, Nina
Simone and others.

And I've fallen under it
Happily, willingly
Because you delight me,
And confound me;
I dream of our ecstasy, dear Felipe.
I cherish your mystery, dear Diana,
I cherish it more than anything else on this earth,
Even if I do not understand it.
...
How can you be both man and woman,
Sun and moon to me?
What trick is this you play upon me?
What love is it you seek?
I tell you true, I do not know,
But I'm yours
Whether man or woman
You may be.
My soul loves. That is all.
It does not, will not, choose shape or sex,
but rather the majestic grace
of love complete.

Scene 9

Finea (*appears, reading*): What strange words are
these?
Laura: What is it, Finea?
Finea: I found a piece of paper
Floating in one of the fountains.
It's written as if in blood:
'Laura was here once without Diana.'

Laura: Strange words, strange time….
We're all made strange, aren't we?
Finea: Not as strange as this.
Laura: You'd be surprised.
Finea: By what? Tell me.
Or aren't we friends anymore?
Laura: Of course we are.
Finea: After all we've been through.
Laura: I know. Oh, Finea, it's just…if I tell you…
Finea: Yes?
Laura: You have to promise.
Finea: I promise.
Laura: Promise to keep it a secret.
Finea: I will.
Laura: On your life.
Finea: I swear.
Laura: I love…I love my secretary
More than if she were a woman.
Finea: …I was hoping you'd say something like that.
If you don't mind my saying,
The way I saw you two carrying on,
I've often thought she was a man.
Laura: It doesn't shock you.
Finea: Why should it?
A man like that is hard to resist.
He's got beauty, smarts…
If I were in your position, I'd go for him myself.
Laura: Finea!
Finea: Just speaking truth. No offense intended.
Laura: None taken. Just a little…
Finea: Shocked?

Laura: No. No. You're a good friend.

Finea: Loyal and true.

Laura: Yes, well, listen, would you do something for me?

Finea: Just say the word.

Laura: He claims his name is Felipe.

Finea: That's a nice name.

Laura: Sweet, isn't it? Anyway, he has quite a story to tell, very strange, very moving,
But I'm not altogether sure it's true.
You see, the details don't quite fit.
He's lived one kind of life,
(so he says)
But behaves sometimes
as if he's lived another.
I want to be his wife.
I'm ready and willing,
but... I need proof.

Finea: That he's what he says he is.

Laura: Exactly. So, would you...Would you pretend to seduce him for me?

Finea: It'd be my pleasure. Thing is....

Laura: What?

Finea: What if things get, you know...?

Laura: What?

Finea: Out of hand.

Laura: How could they get out of hand
If all you'll be doing is acting,
Playing a part?

Finea: Well, you know how acting is....
Sometimes when you're playing a role

It can get quite real.

Laura: It won't.

Finea: … I'll be a good actor. Don't worry.

As soon as I'm satisfied, I'll make my exit.

Laura: Go on, then, Finea.

Set yourself upon the stage.

Finea: Love, love, your theatre is sublime.

Laura: Transcendent in its mystery.

Exit Laura. Finea remains.

Finea: Oh God, I'm not fit for this stage.

All eyes are upon me (I can feel them)

What do I do? What role do I play?

Sure, I'm bold. Sure, I'm brave.

But on my own terms, on my own terrain.

But here? Like this?

How can I meet Diana,

How can I meet Felipe,

And not blush with shame

(Or happiness)

When I finally meet him face to face?

Love is like a child.

It walks blindly, openly, into what it desires.

But what if one doesn't know what one desires?

Love will wound me. It always does.

I'll just have to pray I don't get cut.

Scene 10

Enter Paris and Estacio.

Paris: I am going to tear this riddle up
into a thousand little pieces.
Estacio: Now, Paris, don't give up.
Paris: It's not fair, Estacio!
Why should I have to answer riddles?
Why should I have to debate anything?
Estacio: I'm sure she's doing all this just to stall us.
She's not ready for marriage yet,
So she's come up with this piece of theatre,
To wear you all out and make you go away.
Once you do,
She'll have all the time in the world
to choose a husband.
Paris: It makes me sick. Do you hear me?
Estacio: Loud and clear, sir.
Paris: Who are those people over there?
Estacio: New arrivals,
as if there weren't enough already.

*Enter Camacho in his Marquis disguise and Alejandro
disguised as a valet.*

Camacho: Is that a group of ladies over there?
Alejandro: Seems to be.
Camacho: Well, come on, hand me my eye-glass.
If they are ladies, I need to get a good look at them.

Alejandro hands small binoculars to Camacho.

157

Paris: I wonder who that is.

Estacio: A man with a bad eye, so it seems.

Camacho: I wonder what the ladies around here think of me.

Alejandro: Oh, they're crazy about you.

Camacho: Is that true?

Alejandro: Would I lie to you, sir?

Camacho: No, no, you're a good man. You're an honest man.

Alejandro: That I am.

Camacho: So, what have they told you?

Alejandro: The usual nonsense.

Camacho: Details, please.

Alejandro: That you're amazing, wonderful, exquisite,

Camacho: Yes…?

Alejandro: Charming, unusual,

Camacho: Unusual?

Alejandro: Extraordinary.

Camacho: That's more like it.

Alejandro: And sophisticated. In short: a catch

Camacho: I like the sound of that.
And tell me, all these words, these sweet words…are they really for me?

Alejandro: Apparently.

Camacho: I bet it's my money they're after.

Alejandro: Not from what they say.

Camacho: You mean to tell me…?

Alejandro: Love, sweet love (as the song goes).[7]
That's all they want.

Camacho: Well, if that's all they want....
There's plenty to give. Oh, ladies....!
Estacio: Excuse me.
Alejandro: Yes?
Estacio: My lord wants to know who that man of yours is.
Alejandro: No man of mine; only someone I work for.
Estacio: Yes, well, but who is he?
Alejandro: Can't you tell just by looking at him?
He's none other than Don Lucas of Galicia, the
Marquis of Mal-Odor.
Estacio: And he's come to...?
Alejandro: Court Laura's secretary Diana.
Estacio: Oh. That's great news. I'll tell him right away.
Paris: You don't have to tell me, Estacio,
I've heard it all.
And it's made me hopeful
That a solution is in sight.
Estacio: What do you mean?
Paris: If Diana comes to love this man
as she would a husband,
then the secrets of the labyrinth will be his;
All I have to do is make friends with him,
And he's bound to tell me what he discovers.
After all, men tell each other everything.

•

---

[7] "What the World Needs Now" by Bacharach-David has been recorded by many artists, including Coldplay.

Estacio: Speak to him, then.

Paris: Let me kiss your hands.

Camacho: Who's this?

Alejandro: The Prince of Urbino.

Camacho: Oh, I see.

Forgive me for not recognizing you immediately,

But I've only just arrived,

And I'm afraid my eyesight isn't what it should be.

Paris: I'm not always recognized.

I like it when people don't, actually.

It's nice to be anonymous sometimes.

Camacho: There's more freedom that way.

Paris: What do you mean?

Camacho: To come, do and go as one pleases.

Kiss away, kiss away. You're a brute!

Paris: What?

Alejandro: *(simultaneous)* What?

Estacio: This man is very strange.

Camacho: Tell me, man, why have my gloves been perfumed like this?

Alejandro: Like what?

Camacho: They reek of musk.

Alejandro: I only wanted to temper the smell of myrrh, sir.

Camacho: Temper the myrrh? Temper the myrrh? What do you think I am, eh, brute?

Alejandro: I don't know, sir.

Camacho as Marquis taunts Alejandro as valet with the gloves, using them as physical weapon suffused with erotic energy. The rougher the game, the more to Paris' delight as he watches.

Camacho: You don't know? Well, let me tell you,
I am not a common man.
I am not one bit of a common man.
Do you understand me? Brute?
Alejandro: I get it, sir.
Camacho: Musk, brute,
Musk is common. You hear me?
You are to use it sparingly, discreetly, delicately….
Or it stinks up the place. You follow me?
Alejandro: Stinks. Yes.
Camacho: Musk in good measure, man.
In fine measure, but not like this!
Send this back to the glove-maker immediately.
Paris: He's a demanding Spaniard.
Estacio: He's exactly the kind of man Diana will fall for, too.
Paris: From what we've seen so far
he certainly would seem to be the ideal partner.
So, Marquis, how was the Spanish Court when you left it?
Camacho: Ah, Prince Urbino.
Paris: Please. Call me Paris.
Camacho: Paris? Are you sure?
Paris: Yes.
Camacho: Ah, Paris, well well, the Spanish Court
was…well, but then again, not so well.

Paris: How so?

Camacho: They didn't want me to leave.

That's the truth.

My departure caused a great deal of sadness.

Paris: So, why has your Lordship come all this way?

Camacho: You ask and I answer.

Yes, I will tell you, Paris.

It was the strangest thing.

You see, one day,

right as I was about to go to sleep,

I saw a portrait of Diana.

Paris: Our Diana?

Camacho: The very one.

And I'm sure I don't need to tell you –

As one man to another

(You're a man, aren't you?)

Paris: Yes, sir.

Camacho: Yes. I see.

As you can imagine,

to see a beauty such as Diana's,

especially right before going to sleep,

can send a mind,

Not to mention, a body

(if you get my meaning)

Spinning with desire.

When I woke up, I was determined she'd be my wife.

I'd stop at nothing.

So, here I am, every inch of me

ready and willing,

To make my dream a reality.

Paris: And is your love aware of your intentions?

Camacho: I've had messages sent.

Paris: And she's received them?

Camacho: As far as I know.

Why? You know something I don't?

Paris: No. Just asking. That's all.

Camacho: You put me in doubt.

I don't like to be put in doubt.

It messes up my equilibrium.

What's a man without his equilibrium? I ask you!

Paris: An unbalanced man?

Camacho: Unbalanced. That's right.

And I'll have none of it.

You hear me, brute?

Alejandro: Yes, sir.

Camacho: Take notes! Take notes, man!

Don't idle about. Make yourself useful in this world.

There's enough uselessness to go around.

It's a shame. A real shame.

Throw me off course, I tell you,

but don't unbalance me.

I'm a calm man, Paris.

A calm, even-tempered man.

I refuse doubt to enter my soul.

Paris: I can see that.

Camacho: If I send a message, it gets there, right?

It doesn't get lost or go somewhere else.

If I pride myself on anything,

it's proper messenger service!

Paris: Yes. Well…

By all means, you should marry Diana.

Camacho: Oh, I will. Mark my words. She's the one for me. No question.

Estacio: This is the moment to try and win his friendship.

Paris: Sir, would you…do me the honor of dining with me tonight?

Camacho: What are friends for?
Of course I'll dine with you. Paris, it'd be my honor.
Hey there! Brute!
I'll be dining today with Paris of Urbino;
Tell the Duchess and all the rest
that they shouldn't lose any appetite
on account of me.
I've no doubt this fine gentleman here
will look after me properly.

Paris: Oh, I will, sir.

Camacho: Brute!

Alejandro: What?

Camacho: And don't forget to tell the Duchess to drink to my health, for I'll be drinking to hers…………

Scene 11

As the men exit, enter Finea and Florela.

Florela: What's gotten into you? Why are you flirting with me?

Finea: My lady flirts with you.

Florela: What?

Finea: Laura.

Florela: Laura flirts with me?

Finea: From what I've seen,
You're out in the open.
Why play coy with me?

Florela: I'm a woman.

Finea: So? Where does it say I can't love you?

Florela: You can't love me the way you want.

Finea: What do you mean?

Florela: Your love for me seems more than just
platonic.

Finea: What's wrong with that?
If we think of all the things and creatures
that have inspired the love of humans,
how could we object if a woman loves a woman?

Florela: I, Finea, object to your touching me like this.
Stop. Please.

Finea: But I want you.

Florela: You can't have me.

Finea: But I love you.

Florela: And I love Laura.
She offers me a nobler love than yours. You see?

Finea: And if I were to think of you as a man,
would you stop me then?

Florela: I'm not a man. Do you understand?

Finea: I'm only saying if you were…

Florela: But I'm not. So, enough of this…enough!

Finea: (I'm going to have to sneak into her bedroom

And catch her without her clothes on; that's all there
is to it.) I'm sorry… I just thought…
Florela: You thought wrong.
Finea: Yes, I see that now. Well, shall we be friends,
then?
Florela: Sure. Friends.

Enter Laura, yelling at maid Off.

Laura: No, no, no and a thousand times no.
Just give him back his note.
Florela: What note?
Laura: Oh, it's nothing.
Florela: Tell me, what note? It was from Alejandro,
wasn't it?
Laura: I didn't accept it.
Florela: I'm dead already!
Laura: What is wrong with you?
Florela: I'm fainting.
Laura: Hold my hand.
Florela: Oh!
Finea: As soon as you mentioned who the note was
from, it was as if she'd been struck by lightning.
She didn't act that way with me.
Laura: You found out nothing?
Finea: What is there to find?
You love her.
You never leave her side,
And yet you don't know if she's a man or a woman.
What kind of love is that?
A delusion. Nothing more.

You've wasted enough time, Laura.
She's here now, on the ground, unconscious.
Open her blouse,
And stare at her breasts,
if she has any.
Laura: You're right. I'll take off her clothes.
Florela: Oh my God!
Finea: Careful!
Laura: Darling, are you all right!
Florela: I don't know what came over me.
Did I say anything, Laura, do anything....?
Laura: Finea, why don't you go see what my mother
is up to?
Finea: At once.

Exits.

Laura: My darling Felipe, we're alone now.
Florela: I know, Laura, and I know
what you were trying to do just now.
You should be ashamed of yourself.
Laura: I meant nothing…
Florela: What is it that you want from me?
Or from Alejandro?
If I offended you as a man,
Then I'll go back to being a woman.
I lied to you, Laura; I have lied;
I am woman, can't you see?
If I said I was a man,
it was to only to deceive you temporarily.

Laura: Felipe, there is no more need
to keep inventing things. I don't care anymore.
Whatever sex or creature you might be,
You're my destiny.

Scene 12

Enter the Duchess of Ferrara and Ricardo (as the Infante of Aragon.) Music in the background. The air of a cocktail party.

Duchess: Is that Laura?
Laura: It is, mother.
Duchess: You're joining us, then?
Laura: Of course.
Duchess: That's the spirit. That's what I like to hear.
Everyone: it seems my dear Laura has finally decided
to be seen in public again.
Laura: Mother…
Duchess: Can't I be proud of you?
Laura: Of course, but…
Infante (Ricardo): Dear lady, let me kiss your feet.
Laura: And you are?
Infante : The Infante of Aragon, *mademoiselle.*
Duchess: He's a good man, Laura. Be kind.
Laura: A pleasure to meet you, Infante.
Infante: The pleasure's all mine.
Florela: Pay no attention to me.
Laura: Would you excuse me, sir?
Infante: By all means.

Laura: What's wrong with you? Don't you realize I'm just appeasing my mother?

Florela: And if the Infante had been Alejandro?

Laura: Then I would've run out the door.

Duchess: Infante, you should be near Laura.

Infante: If I may, Diana…

Florela: What?

Infante: *(kisses her hand)* The Infante of Aragon, *mademoiselle.*

Florela: Are you sure?

Infante: Absolutely.

Enter Camacho.

Camacho: Forgive me, your Excellency, for being so late. I was held up by another Duchess.
You know how these things are. Busy, busy.
But I'm here now,
At your service, as it were,
Ready and willing
And most honored to kiss your illustrious feet.

Laura: He's an interesting fellow.

Infante: *(aside)* He's an interesting scoundrel, that's for sure.

Duchess: Your Lordship is a thousand times welcome. Some more seats, please!

Camacho: *(working the room; a player in his natural orbit)* Oh, I can sit anywhere. I'm flexible. Don't trouble yourself over me. May I kiss your hand, fair lady?

Laura: You may.

Florela: *(aside)* His lips are on her hand, but his eyes are on me. I don't know what to make of this.

Camacho: And you are, I take it, the famous Diana?

Florela: Hardly famous, but certainly Diana. I answer only to the Grand Duchess and my Lady Laura.

Camacho: Your portraits don't do you justice, Diana. No. You're more beautiful

Than anyone had ever led me to believe.

Florela: You're bold, sir.

Camacho: I'm how you want me.

Florela: *(aside)* It seems this man is also guided by love's possibilities.

Infante: I say, Your Highness?

Duchess: What is it, young man?

Infante: I take it you'll make this gentleman's stay here worthwhile, then?

Duchess: It is my hope that everyone feels welcome in my house.

Camacho: *(to a page:)* You there!

Go fetch the present I brought for her Excellency.

Infante: Is it some rare object?

Camacho: No, just a mere trifle:

A marble and jasper fountain.

Here it is now.

I had to have it shipped in different sections,

Otherwise it wouldn't fit.

But once it's put together, you'll see,

What a splendid fountain it is.

The fountain is readily assembled. It is a grand, but not gaudy, phallic enterprise.

Duchess: I see you're a man of taste and presence.
Camacho: I do what I can.
Duchess: No doubt we'll find an excellent home for it. Marquis, it'd be a great pleasure if you would dine with me.
Camacho: It'd be my honor, ma'am.
Infante: Good night, then.
Duchess: There's no need for you to go, Infante; Come. Dine with us.
Infante: It'd be my honor, ma'am.
Duchess: You'll sit next to me, Marquis; I am relying on you to cheer me up.
Camacho: I'll do my best, ma'am.

Exit all but Laura and Florela

Scene 13

Laura: Are you still angry with me?
Florela: My love for you won't let me stay angry.
If only I could go back to being a woman,
then everything would be fine; I'd just be Diana,
your humble servant Diana.
But as a man, which is what I really am,
how can I not kill myself knowing
there's nothing I can do or say
that will stop you from seeing Alejandro tonight?
Laura: Felipe, if you really don't want me to see him,

Then why don't you go instead?
You can pretend that you're me.
And that way
you can tell Alejandro anything you want.
Florela: You're so kind to me, and I've been…
I've behaved…so foolishly. What must you think of
me?
Laura: I think you find being a man quite a burden.
Florela: Not at all. How else could I have you as my
wife?

Florela kisses Laura passionately. A moment.

Laura: *(aside)* He is a man then! All I need now is
proof!

Laura goes within.

Florela: *(aside; alone)* If only I were a man.

Act Three

Scene 14

*Night. Florela and Laura are on the terrace. Alejandro
appears below.*

Florela: That looks like Alejandro.
Laura: Go on, then. Speak to him. You have my
blessing.
Florela: What about you?

Laura: I'll wait for you in the corridor;
I know you'll do well by me.

Laura exits.

Florela: I can't believe she's left me alone.
Hello? Who goes there?
Are you Alejandro?
Alejandro: I am.
Florela: The same Alejandro
Who, in Mantua, is said to have loved Florela?
Alejandro: Who?
Florela: Have you forgotten her already?
You promised to marry her.
Alejandro: Florela? I didn't promise anything.
Look, whoever told you this is lying,
And wants you to hate me.
Florela: *(Aside)* I should just tell him who I am
And get this charade over with.
But if I do, everything I've built so far
Will come crashing to the ground.
And then what?
Laura finds out that I'm a woman,
And she'll head straight into Alejandro's arms.
Alejandro: There are people coming; I'll be back later.

Alejandro hides. Florela goes within. Enter Camacho, with a lantern.

Camacho: Seduced and abandoned: that's me.
The Duchess asleep,

The Infante off somewhere,
And what do I get?
A rough embrace and off she goes
Back into the dark.
I didn't even get a proper kiss from Finea.
Alejandro: Who goes there?
What are you doing with that light?
Put it out. Get the hell out of here.
Camacho: I'm not going anywhere.
I don't care who you are.
Nobody talks to me like that.
Alejandro: If you don't tell me who you are,
I will grab you and your lantern
and hurl both of you clear across the garden.
Camacho: I am Don Lucas, the Marquis de Mal-odor!
Alejandro: You're not Camacho?
Camacho: You're not Alejandro?
Alejandro: You're insane. What the hell are you doing here?
Camacho: I had you, didn't I? You were scared out of your wits!
Alejandro: I was not.
Camacho: Were too. I heard it in your voice.
(mocking) "Put it out. Get the hell out of here"
Alejandro: Keep your voice down. She'll hear you.
Camacho: Who?
Alejandro: Laura. She's on the balcony.
Camacho: She is?
Alejandro: And so is Diana, I suspect.
Camacho: Diana? Diana, it's me, your noble suitor!
I am waiting here by the light of the moon.

Just say the word and paradise will be yours.

Florela: *(appearing)* Who is that?

Camacho: The Marquis Don Lucas.

Florela: You're early. I can't talk to you now.
But your sweet words deserve some reward.

Camacho: Whatever token you can spare
I will cherish with all my heart.

Florela: I've written something to you,
But you must tell me first.
Are you as discreet as Laura says you are?

Camacho: No man was ever more discreet than I.

Florela: Well, here it is. Goodbye.

Camacho: Stay.

Florela: I cannot. *(she goes within)*

Alejandro: Is she gone?

Camacho: Yes. Diana's gone.

Alejandro: And Laura?

Camacho: She was already inside.

Alejandro: What did she give you?

Camacho: Another fucking piece of paper!

Alejandro: Lucky you.

Camacho: Lucky nothing. I deserve a hell of a lot
more for my trouble.

Alejandro: Read it. You've brought a light, after all.

Camacho: Read it now?

Alejandro: It's as good a time as any.

Camacho: What is it with you and reading, eh?

Alejandro: What?

Camacho: You like being read to, don't you?

Alejandro: Just read it!

Camacho: *reading:* 'I love the one who loves me not,

I do not love the one who loves me'
Alejandro: Go on.
Camacho: That's it.
Alejandro: What do you mean that's it?
Camacho: Just what I said. That's all there is.
Alejandro: Well, what does it mean?
Camacho: Isn't it obvious?
She loves me, but she thinks I don't love her;
She loves me so much
She's even rejected other potential suitors.
Alejandro: You're delusional.
Camacho: I'm delusional all right.
I'm so delusional I've even found
A way of sneaking into the labyrinth
With enough supplies to last
Us a month if you need.
Alejandro: How'd you manage that?
Camacho: Simple. I gave the Duchess a gift.
A splendid fountain, if I do say so myself.
And she's done exactly as I thought she would.
She's had the pieces placed in the small courtyard
Right at the entrance to the labyrinth.
As the fountain is assembled, I'll be able
To hide some fine wines, cheeses
And delicious cakes inside of it.
I figure even if you lose yourself,
you'll have enough to live on for a good long time.
Alejandro: You're a genius! I love you.
Camacho: No need to get overexcited now.
Alejandro: The day we met was the luckiest day of
my life. I want you to know that.

Camacho: …that's very nice.

Alejandro: I mean it. Camacho…

Camacho: Someone's coming. We should get out of here.

Alejandro: Which way?

Camacho: Just follow my lead, and Laura will be yours, my friend, or my name isn't the Marquis de Mal-odor.

Scene 15

The Duchess, Ricardo as the Infante, Laura, Finea, Paris, Estacio and Florela enter, perhaps accompanied by music. Florela takes her seat behind a table. Alejandro and Camacho stay behind a bit.

Florela: Gracious Duchess, noble princes,
And everyone else gathered here today,
I ask you to forgive me
In advance for not making the sort of speech
One should at an occasion such as this.

Alejandro: My eyes must be playing tricks on me.

Camacho: What are you talking about?

Alejandro: That's not Diana.

Camacho: What do you mean?

Alejandro: That's Florela.

Camacho: Who?

Alejandro: Florela, Florela….

Camacho: Shh. She's staring at us.

Alejandro: The whole world can stare at us for all I care. This is nothing but a game.

Camacho: I thought you liked games.

Alejandro: I like an even playing field. But not this: All Florela is doing is meddling
In other people's happiness.

Camacho : Shh. She's about to say something.

Florela: And now to the subject of our debate today:

Alejandro and Camacho come in.

Alejandro: Some debate.

Florela: What's that?

Alejandro: Nothing. Go on, Diana.
Your name is Diana, isn't it?

Florela: And you are - ?

Alejandro: You know exactly who I am.

Duchess: Are you all right, young man?

Alejandro: Yes, of course. Sorry. I must be nervous.

Duchess: Eager to get started. That's a good sign.
Don't you think, Laura?

Laura: Yes. Most definitely.

Paris: Oh, I'm eager too.

Infante: As am I.

Camacho: Me too. I'm nothing but eager.

Florela: Well, I'm delighted you are all so incredibly eager. I'm sure Laura is equally appreciative.

Laura: I'm quite interested in what all of you have to say.

Florela: So, there you have it: there will be no animosity here.

Alejandro: (Wanna bet?)

Florela: This is to be a friendly debate. A fair debate.
And nothing more. Is that understood?

Paris, Infante, Camacho: Yes.

Florela: Alejandro?

Alejandro: Yes. Yes.

Florela: Let us begin.
The topic on the floor today is:
Are women as equally capable as men
in matters of government, war, and the sciences?
To which I posit: a resounding yes.

Alejandro: Rebuttal.

Florela: Excuse me?

Alejandro: I'm afraid I would have to disagree with
you, Diana. That is your name, isn't it? Diana?

Florela: Yes.

Alejandro: I'm sure it's a very useful name.
The kind of name women use to seduce men,
To make them believe they're in love with them.

Florela: I've never made anyone believe anything.
From what I understand,
it's always the other way around.
A man will say anything to seduce a woman.

Alejandro: From what you understand or what you
know, Diana?

Florela: Your point?

Alejandro: My point? My point is that women are
imperfect beings.
They mess things up. Why?
Because they weren't part of the plan
In the first place.

Florela: What plan is that?

Alejandro: The divine plan. You know, Adam and Eve and all that way back when.

Florela: I didn't know you were the religious type.

Alejandro: I'm full of faith.

Florela: But you're not faithful.

Alejandro: I didn't say that.

Florela: (You don't have to.)

Infante: If I may, Diana…

I've some words that might elucidate this debate.

Florela: Go on.

Infante: Women…

Florela: Yes.

Infante: Women are…

Duchess: …I think his eagerness is getting the best of him at the moment.

Laura: I think it's charming.

Infante: Women…

Camacho: …Are divine creatures. God bless them. That's the truth.

Is that what you were going to say?

Infante: Well, actually I…

I can't remember what I was going to say.

I've lost my train of thought.

Camacho: It'll come back to you… don't worry.

Alejandro: What he was going to say was that they were not divine at all. Isn't that right?

Infante: No.

Alejandro: Adam was first. He didn't need Eve.

He doesn't need Eve

To follow him wherever he goes.

Florela: Who says she's following?

Alejandro: I see it with my own eyes.

Florela: Your eyes deceive you.

Alejandro: I'm not blind. I know what I see.

Florela: What is it you see?

Alejandro: A woman.

Florela: Are you sure?

Alejandro: There's not a woman who can hide from me.

Florela: You're awfully sure of yourself.

Alejandro: Is it a crime to be confident?

Florela: You're not on trial here.

Alejandro: But if I were…?

Florela: Which you're not.

Alejandro: But if I were…

Florela: The quality of confidence is not exclusive to men.

Alejandro: It's more attractive in a man, though.

Florela: Unless it's used against women.

Alejandro: I'm not against women. I love women.

Florela: How many?

Camacho: I think this is a splendid debate.
Really, it puts me in mind
Of my cousins in Gibraltar –
yes, they're always debating
Making points, turning the tide.
I like my cousins. I do.
Especially because it's so precipitous in Gibraltar.
Any wrong move and you're off a cliff,
you know what I mean?
But they're good debaters.

181

Very, very confident debaters.

I think confidence is a key quality. In any one.

It should not be underestimated by any means.

Alejandro: What does Eve want to follow Adam around for, clear across to another city,

When it's evident she's never been part of Nature's original design?

Florela: If she wasn't part of Nature's original design, as you so gracelessly put it,

Then what use has Adam to toy with Eve,

To beg her affection,

seduce her, and shower her with compliments?

Camacho: Women like compliments. That's the truth.

Alejandro: That's not what we're talking about!

Florela: No, actually,

we're talking about women's role in society

And what they're capable of

and what men think they're not capable of.

Paris: I think women are quite capable.

Florela: Really?

Paris: Oh. Yes. In their place. You know.

Florela: Their place? What place is that?

Paris: Well, I mean it's a question of predisposition, really.

Florela: Would you care to expand?

Paris: Well, if I may, I think women…

Florela: Yes?

Infante: I remember now.

Florela: What?

Infante: What I was going to say. I remember.

Paris : You're always interrupting me.

Infante: I am not.

Paris: You are too. Every time I try to say something, you –

Infante: I barely know you.

Paris: Precisely. So, why don't you -?

Florela: Infante? Infante? Go on.

Infante: Yes, thank you.

If I may be so bold, Diana,

Just this once…

Florela: What is it, Infante?

Infante: I've always been on women's side.

Even when in the company of men,

It is women I defend.

Women are… divine. Yes. As this good man says.

But they are also infinitely complex

And rewarding of all patience.

Even when they think less of themselves,

As so often they do, it is sad for me to say,

they remain,

Indeed, they are

…the greatest compass to the heart.

Florela: …I don't know what to say.

Infante: You don't need to say anything.

They're just words, Diana. Words from a soldier

Who has kept watch patiently

During times of distress and despair.

Camacho: And joy too. Am I right?

Infante: Of course.

Laura: He's rather sweet, isn't he?

Duchess: The Infante shows a great deal of promise.

Paris: Yes, well, this is all very well…

But look, let's base this argument in fact,

Not illusion. In science, not fiction.

Tell me, Diana,

which is the most important part of the body?

Florela: There are so many ways I could answer this,

But I'd have to say the heart is the most vital organ.

Paris: Right. So, if the body can be divided up into

More important and less important organs

so too can the soul.

Certain areas, shall we say, of the soul

Are more inclined and less inclined

Toward certain things.

It's a matter of predisposition.

Women just don't have the temperament for science.

Florela: With what confidence you dive into your argument!

Paris: I've always prided myself in my confidence.

Alejandro: As have I.

Florela: Then tell me this, Paris,

which humor is best suited to the intellect?

Paris: Humor?

Florela: It's old-fashioned I know, but humor me, if you would.

Paris: It'd be my pleasure. To the intellect, you said?

Florela: Yes. Which humor is best suited to the intellect?

Paris: Well, after careful thought,
I'd have to say, without question,
the melancholic humor.
Florela: Why's that?
Paris: Old people. They're wise, right?
Because sadness is their dominant humor.
Camacho: Now I know why I'm always so sad.
It's damned wisdom bringing me down.
(But if the saddest people are the wisest,
Does that mean the poorest people
Are the greatest geniuses of all?)
Florela: Wisdom can also come from experience.
It doesn't depend on being melancholy.
Alejandro: I sustain wisdom comes
from being left alone.
Nothing is better for a person than to be let go.
Florela: To be abandoned?
Alejandro: To be let go. There's a difference.
Florela: Even at the expense of what's transpired
between them, what's been promised?
Alejandro: What men promise
and what men do are two different things.
That's what women don't understand.
Florela: Hence that makes them what?
Inferior in your eyes?
Alejandro: Foolish, that's all. (Fools in love.)
Florela: Weak?
Alejandro: I didn't say that.
Florela: You reiterate clichés; you are a cliche.
Alejandro: Women want too much.
Venus and Mars. Okay?

If you want clichés, let's drag them out, then.
Eve, born <u>out</u> of design, seeks to be with Adam.
Adam seeks to follow his own path,
the path he began without Eve.
He doesn't want to be distracted.
But he falls in for a moment,
He gives in.
Florela: He gives too much.
Alejandro: He promises things. Yes.
Words fly out of his mouth
Because in the moment they seem right
Florela: Seem, but not are.
Alejandro: Things seem as they seem. What is there
to question?
Florela: What's true.
Alejandro: Truth is an illusion. You know that better
than anyone.
Florela: And these words that fly so swiftly out of his
mouth? What is Eve to make of them?
Are words not actions, after all?
Is Adam not to be held accountable for his actions?
Alejandro: Words are words. They suit the
circumstance.
Florela: You think the human heart can be played
with?
Alejandro: I think women's hearts are less sturdy
than men's.
Florela: Your point is not only ridiculous,
But scientifically insane.
Without women and their "rickety" hearts,
humanity would not exist,

And we would not even be here today
having this argument.
Duchess: Isn't she clever?
Alejandro: You misinterpret me.
Florela: In what way do I misinterpret you?
Tell me, Alejandro.
...
Your argument, such as it is,
Ill-formed, ill-advised, and sketchy in its execution,
No doubt driven out of guilt
and a fair bit of incredulity
At what Eve is indeed capable of,
Capable and more, if she's let
(and she will be let),
is nothing more than a demonstration of
Your blind, arrogant prejudice.
Camacho: Well-put, Diana.
There will be no arguments to that.
I won't allow them.
It's clear, as it always should have been,
That men and women are equal.
I could go on and on about women:
Their grace, sophistication, insight, perception,
Depth of knowledge, and so on,
But if I have to say one thing in their defense:
If any one here persists in calling women imperfect,
I will have to resolve this conflict
By what are commonly deemed traditional male
means: Namely, a duel.
Full-out, no holds barred, may the best man win.
I've had enough of this nonsense.

If anyone wants a fight, see me in my country estate.
If I'm in a good mood, I'll be lying stone drunk
under the shadow of a tree;
if I'm not, I'll be at home,
having a good meal,
the kind all men and women deserve,
and if you can't find me at the table,
then you'll find me in bed,
snoring a peaceful snore to my heart's content.

Exit Camacho.

Duchess: Stop him. Don't let him get away.
Laura: It's too late; I don't think he'll be coming back.
Duchess: The debate is over.
Gentlemen, go on now. The labyrinth awaits you.

Exit everyone except Alejandro.

Alejandro: Anyone want to be in my shoes?
I'll be happy to give them away.
God knows no one could be more unhappy than I am
right now.
I leave Florela in Mantua
 - quiet and tearful as a rose.
Only to find her in Ferrara
 - Relentless as an avenging angel.

Enter Camacho.

Camacho: What's this? Tears?

Alejandro: No.

Camacho: I should say not. You've work to do, my friend. There's the damned labyrinth to deal with.

Alejandro: I should go straight back to Ferrara.
I'm only making a fool of myself here.
Florela has certainly seen to it
That Laura will never be mine.

Camacho: All the more reason, then, to get in her way. You can't let her stop you
From pursuing Laura, and your destiny.

Alejandro: My love for her will be the end of me;
but for her sake I am prepared to
die a thousand times…

Camacho: I've heard that before.
Listen, just remember I've placed the fake fountain
in the labyrinth's foyer;
You'll find a little keyhole in the sculpted panel,
turn the key, and everything will be revealed
-lamps, wine, bread, cheese –
Take what you need;
Don't be frugal on my account.
Just take, and you'll be on your way.

Alejandro: I wish you would come in with me. I'd like the company.

Camacho: Oh, that's sweet of you to say, but -

Alejandro: My feelings for you aren't important all of a sudden?

Camacho: You wound me, sir. Straight to the heart.
Of course your feelings matter.
They matter very much.

What would I do without your feelings for me?
You think about that?
Oyster without his shell. That's what I'd be.
No, it's nothing to do with that.
It's just – what if I got to Laura before you did?
Alejandro: Don't worry,
You won't. I'll make sure of it.
We'll just stay together
Until we're almost there
And then we'll split up.
I'll seek her out, and you'll go on your way.
Camacho: This is a rotten deal, if you ask me,
But God knows why, I'll take it. Let's go.
Alejandro: I'll go first.
Camacho: Go on then, but if I'm left behind
In that damned labyrinth,
You better send a letter to Toledo
And let everybody know what happened to me.
A man like me only comes around once every
hundred years.
Why, if right is as right does,
my brain should be donated to science.
That's the truth.
Generations should study my capacity for ingenuity.
I deserve a proper eulogy for my sacrifice:
A fine service
with a dozen choirs singing
A hymn composed especially for the occasion,
Flowers and flowers of all sorts lining the streets,
Bells ringing every hour on the hour
Until the dark of night,

when the sweet sound of birds blends
into the fragrant thick of sleep.
All this and more is due me, you hear?
You hear me?

Exit Camacho and Alejandro.

Scene 16

Enter Laura, Florela, and the Duchess of Ferrara, followed by Finea.

Florela: If I may, Your Excellency,
Would it be possible not to leave the vestibule just
yet?
Duchess: Is there something troubling you?
Florela: Yes, there is.
I don't like the looks of this fountain.
I think there might be something inside it.
Duchess: As I recall, it comes in sections.
We'll just have it taken apart,
and see whether it's made of marble or of treachery.
Finea: Do you think it's rigged?
I wouldn't be surprised if it was.
After all, it was given to us by that strange beast:
the Marquis of Mal-Odor.
Florela: I didn't like him from the moment I set eyes
on him.
Finea: This fountain is so light. I can almost lift it.
Laura: When I saw only two people carrying it, I
thought it couldn't be made of marble or jasper.

Duchess: There seems to be a small crack
Right down the middle here…
Finea: Isn't that a keyhole?
Florela: See if you can pry the whole thing open.
Finea: There, I've got it.
Florela: Is it marble?
Finea: More like Formica.
Florela: So my suspicions were justified.

Finea: Look what we got here. Lanterns, matches, a sparkler…
Duchess: I can't believe it.
Finea: A bottle of wine: Domaine Rothschild, no less. And a ham. A whole ham.
Florela: Here are some jars.
Finea: Full of food. What's he stocking up for? Armageddon?
Florela: This is crazy.
Laura: You have to admire his ingenuity, though.
Duchess: Ingenuity? It's trickery. That's all it is.
Laura: Thank heaven Diana is here. She's outwitted him.
Duchess: I want everything inside the fountain
 to be cleared away at once.

Exit the Duchess, followed by Finea.

Scene 17

Florela: Oh, Laura, I think our days together are
coming to an end.

Laura: Why do you say that?

Florela: Because love will always find a way
through the darkest labyrinth;
there's nothing more ingenious than love.

Laura: No one can take away what we have.
I'll always be yours, Felipe.
If not, I would die.

Florela: So would I.
(I never thought I'd say this, but)
I'm yours completely.
You hold my life in your hands, dear Laura.
If I had an infinite number of souls,
I would have them threaded through your eyelashes
So they could guard your eyes forever.
I'm lost in you;
And that's what I want. to be lost in you,
Everything I've done has been for you:
To keep you near me.
But now…any one of these suitors could reach you,
And where will I be?
Turn him away, Laura.
Please, if he finds you, turn him away.

Laura: I love you. Trust me.

Florela: Another person's love can never be trusted
unless it's equal to or greater than one's own.

Laura: Then it's your love that is unequal,
for no one could love someone as much as I love you.

Florela: But how do you love me?
Laura: As your wife.

Laura kisses Florela passionately.

Scene 18

Enter Finea.

Finea: You two sure do carry on!
I've never seen such a love.
Not even in the middle of a labyrinth
Can you restrain yourselves!
Laura: Go now, and see if there any other surprises in store for us.
Florela: I will.

Exit Florela.

Finea: Laura, listen to me,
it won't be long before you have to marry.
So, you're going to have to stop loving this Felipe or
Whatever she or he calls himself.
Laura: You still haven't told me what happened last night.
Finea: I've been too embarrassed to tell.
Laura: Really?
Finea: I can't believe my daring.
I went right up to his bed
and lifted the silk bedspread.

Laura: What?

Finea: I knew you'd be shocked. But I did it. I couldn't help myself.

Laura: And…?

Finea: As soon as I touched the bedspread,
he stirred, and muttered:
"Is that my Laura,
The one who waits me in the labyrinth of desire?"
"No," I whispered while
Sneaking an eyeful….

Laura: Yes?

Finea: …of his feet.

Laura: Is that all?

Finea: Isn't that enough? He has beautiful feet.

Laura: Finea, just looking at his feet doesn't tell me what I want to know.

Finea: Doesn't it?

Laura: What else did you see or touch?

Finea: I thought you wanted proof.
A woman's feet are very different from a man's.
And that's that.

Laura: The Duchess is calling.

Finea: I'll say no more, then. I've said enough already.

Laura: Answer me one thing: Can I love this person?

Finea: It's not impossible.

Exit Laura and Finea.

Scene 19

Enter Alejandro and Camacho.

Alejandro: For the sheer glory of winning my lady's hand, I'm about to do the most foolish
And dangerous thing in my life.
Camacho: Everything's worth a try, that's my motto.
I'm going in.
Give me light and wine, and some fine slices of ham,
just don't give me any problems! That's all I ask.

Exit Camacho and Alejandro. Enter Estacio and Paris.

Estacio: Don't go in, please!
Paris: Of course I'm going in.
Estacio: Sir, how could you possibly go in just like that? It's a labyrinth.
Paris: So?
Estacio: What if you never find your way out?
Paris: Don't worry about me. I've all I need right here.
You see this sword?
Estacio: Yes.
Paris: Take it out of its sheath.
Estacio: I love the feel of cold steel on my hands.
Paris: There's more to it than that.
Estacio: Oh?
Paris: There's a candle in there.
It runs the whole length of the blade.
The hilt is hollow;
All I have to do is turn a screw
And… I've all I need to start a flame.

Estacio: What if the flame burns out?
Paris: I've anticipated that already, which is why I
found out the secret code.
Estacio: How'd you - ?
Paris: Money helped.
Estacio: You're amazing.
Paris: So long, Estacio.

Enter Infante.

See you in the palace.

Exit Paris.

Infante: He'll see me first.
Estacio: What's that?
Infante: There's no man readier for the labyrinth
Than I.
Estacio: Have you figured it out, then?
Infante: No, but I've this jacket here.
Fits me well, doesn't it?
Estacio: It's quite nice.
Infante: Go on. Touch. Silk. That's right, and this
braid here is pure gold.
Estacio: Really?
Infante: I wouldn't lie to you.
I'm not like that. I don't like lies.
Now, this braid – if I prick it,
Gently, right here,
It will come undone,
And when it does

197

It will form a single, brilliant ball of thread
That will lead my way
Through the labyrinth
Just as you suggested.
Estacio: You remembered.
Infante: I never forget a kind word or kind gesture
towards me. You're a good man, Estacio. See you at
the palace.
Estacio: May the best man win.

Exit all.

Scene 20

Enter Alejandro, lost inside the labyrinth.

Alejandro: Where in God's name am I?
I've done nothing but wander about,
Go here and there,
And to what end?
I'm back where I'm started.
Or maybe I'm at another entrance
To somewhere else.
No. No. Nothing here.
I'm lost. That's clear.
I should've never trusted Camacho.
He's a riddle all unto his own.
Un-riddle him, and then I'd see the light.
Christ, where am I?
You've really done it this time, Florela.
You wanted to see me suffer?

Well, here I am.
I'm suffering like an idiot
In this shit labyrinth.
Dear God in Heaven, have mercy on me.

Enter Camacho, also lost.

Camacho: So much for the lamps and sparklers.
They must have found them before me.
There's not a thing left.
Not even a piece of cheese.
I tell you, is that any way to treat a man?
To leave him in the dark,
in misery and hunger?
Fucking sadist made this labyrinth!
I don't like suffering. You hear me?
It doesn't turn me on!
Where the hell am I?
Dear God, I'm going to die, and it's all my own fault!
Alejandro: I hear voices.
Camacho: And for what? A bottle of wine.
Alejandro: They sound familiar.
Camacho: I'm starting to hear voices.
This is it. I'm nearing the end.
Alejandro: It's closer now.
Don't lose the voice, Alejandro.
Camacho: If this is the end, dear God,
I've been a good man, an honest man
Most of the time.
I've done what I had to do to get by.
Have pity on me.

I don't pray very often, but I'm praying now
You hear me?
End my torment now.
Let me rest in peace.
Alejandro: Oh, sweet Laura,
I knew you'd take pity on me.
Camacho: Could it be Laura's sweet voice I hear?
Oh, if it be so….
Alejandro: If it is her….
Camacho: My dear Laura,
Alejandro: I am yours.

The two embrace.

Camacho: Oh, to be finally in your arms.
Alejandro: Who are you?
Camacho: Don Lucas. Who are you?
Alejandro: Alejandro, you idiot.
Camacho: I thought it was Laura.
Alejandro: If it only it was Laura…
This is all your fault.
Camacho: How was I to know they'd shift everything around?
Alejandro: It was your fountain, Camacho.
Camacho: Yes, it was. But apparently, your clever lady love didn't like it and got rid of it.
Alejandro: You could've said something!
I mean, if you saw it was gone, why did you come in?

Camacho: To look for you.
Alejandro: And what do we do now?
Camacho: Got anything to eat?
Alejandro: Only the glorious food
That was supposed to be in the fountain.
Camacho: I should have known better than to get
myself into a labyrinth!
What was I thinking?
World's enough of a labyrinth already
And look where it's got me?
Stuck inside another one.
Like a fool.
Which is what I am at day's end.
Nothing but a fool,
Following his heart.
Alejandro: Will you stop?
Camacho: Why should I? What else is there to do
But contemplate life
And what it's dealt us?
And we've been dealt, haven't we,
Quite a blow, the two of us.
Alejandro: Shh!
Camacho: What?
Alejandro: I hear voices
Camacho: You too?
Alejandro: Other voices.

Enter Ricardo as the Infante, also lost

Infante: The golden thread has got me nowhere.
I'm as lost as the Minotaur,

And neither sound nor fury will get me out of here.

Camacho: It's a woman's voice. I'm sure of it.

Alejandro: Is it?

Infante: Oh, woe, woe, woe….

Camacho: Definitely.

Alejandro: Very well then, you go that way and I'll follow the voice. Laura, darling, is that you?

Infante: Oh, sweet angel, light of my life!

Alejandro: You can't imagine

What I've gone through searching for you.

Infante: I imagine only too well, my dear.

What's this? Are you a man?

Alejandro: Yes, and I think you're one too.

Infante: I am a man.

Alejandro: What man?

Infante: The Infante.

Camacho: Well, aren't they a pair?

Alejandro: I'm Alejandro.

Camacho: And I'm the Marquis, lover extraordinaire.

Alejandro: Where are you going?

Infante: I'm lost.

Alejandro: We're all going to die here!

Infante: You mean, you can't find the way out either?

Alejandro: I think the only thing we can do at this point is to shout.

Infante: To cave in. I'm with you there.

We've been martyrs for love long enough. Laura!

Alejandro: Laura!

Camacho: Laura!

Infante: Laura!

Alejandro: Laura!

They continue shouting as they disappear in the endless darkness of the labyrinth.

Scene 21

Enter Duchess, Finea, Florela, Laura.

Duchess: No one can find us.
Laura: And I doubt they will.
Duchess: It's amazing.
Laura: This has proved to be quite a test.
Florela: You'd think at least one person
Would see things through to the end,
Especially knowing that Laura's hand is to be won.
Duchess: I pray one of the three men succeeds.
Someone must be worthy of Laura's love.
Florela: I'm so scared I'll lose you.
Laura: Our love for each other will never be broken;
Don't worry.
Florela: I hear voices.

Enter Paris with his lit sword. He is dangerously delirious in his happiness at winning. Perhaps a gloatingly entitled tantrum.

Paris: Well, I'm here.
(Goodbye, my light, I don't need you anymore.)
Why do you all look so surprised?
Don't you recognize me? I'm Paris of Urbino.

Duchess: Who would've thought…?
Paris: Destiny. Plain and simple. I am destined to be Laura's husband.

The shouts of the other mean are heard offstage.

Alejandro: Oh, Laura!
Infante: Laura!
Camacho: Laura! Where are you?
Duchess: There are people lost outside;
Finea, give them light.
Now that the contest is over,
we can help them through the labyrinth.
Laura: Tell me, who gave you that light?
Paris: You did. Your radiance shined through all the paths of the labyrinth.
Laura: I thought you'd been searched.
Paris: I was, but no one thought to look inside my sword.
Dear Laura, give me your hand. Now.
Laura: Wait.

Enter Alejandro, Infante and Camacho.

Alejandro: I thought I was going to die.
Infante: So did I.
Camacho: I thought I was dead already.
Paris: Oh, nice to see you all. Pity you've lost. I got here first.
Alejandro: Don't worry, I surrender.

Infante: As do I.

Camacho: And I, although I admit I don't like surrendering. But rules are rules, right?

Duchess: So they are, and being so, let me not delay this any longer, and give my Laura's hand to Paris, who has rightfully claimed her..

Alejandro: And may they enjoy a thousand years of happiness.

Paris: Give me your hand, Laura

Laura: I can't.

Paris: What do you mean?

Laura: I'm already married.

Paris: What?

Camacho: I see that the labyrinth isn't over yet.

Duchess: Laura, what are you saying? Give your hand this instant.

Laura: No.
I already have a husband. Can't you see?

Duchess: Where is he?

Laura: Here.

Paris: Which one among you is it? Speak now or I'll do you all in.

Alejandro: Don't look at me.

Infante: Nor me, Paris.

Paris: Well, who is it?

Camacho: Stop waving your sword, Paris, this Marquis is in no mood for a duel.

Paris: Anyone who's gone ahead and married Laura is a traitor.

Alejandro: Don't look at me.

Infante: Nor me.

Paris: Then it must be you, dear Marquis…

Camacho: Now, now, if it's me she loves,
Whose fault is that? I'm irresistible.
Come on, let's shake hands. No harm done.

Paris: I would rather kill one hundred Spaniards than
shake your hand.

Camacho: Diana, please tell us
who your husband is,
before we all lose our heads.

Laura: My husband…
Is my secretary.

Duchess: What?

Laura: Diana's a man, and is endowed
with many manly attributes.

Duchess: Are you really a man, Diana?

Florela: I…

Duchess: Speak up, woman…man…

Pause.

Alejandro: Laura, I'm afraid you've been deceived.
If she won't tell you, I will.
You see, Diana is my fiancée.
All these little games we've been playing
Have been devised by her to stop me from marrying
you. Her real name is Florela.

Laura: Felipe, is this true?

Florela: From this moment on
I am no longer Felipe, or Diana.
I am simply Florela.
Forgive me, Laura, please forgive me
For I do love you;
But yes, the truth is,
If we must admit it,
and stop playing these silly,
yet delicious little games,
Is that I came here, driven by jealousy
And all I wanted to do was
to do whatever I needed to do
To win Alejandro
I deceived you and betrayed you all
Just to win his hand.
All I ask is that you to forgive me
Please, Laura…

Laura faints. A moment. Duchess revives her, helps her up.
Laura is weeping; she is devastated.

Laura: Paris, you must forgive me.

Paris: I do.

Laura: I've been a fool.

Florela: No, you've been true. Always.

Camacho: …I've got it. I've got it.

Alejandro: What?

Camacho: The riddle. The answer is you, isn't it
Florela?

Florela: Yes. I was the person, who,

as the riddle said, is and yet is not,
who loves the person whom she does not love.
I was Felipe, and yet not Felipe;
and as for the rest, well,
we've had enough riddles for one day.
Camacho: Oh, does that mean there'll be no more
changing of sex?
You'll marry Alejandro and that's it?
Florela: If he'll have me.
Alejandro: I will.
Florela: After all this, you'll have me?
Alejandro: Yes.
Florela: And I'll have you
just like that, eh?
Alejandro: Florela…
Florela: I love our games, Alejandro. I do.
I love how we play with each other.
But as I stand here, I'm not sure anymore
Even after all this
After all we've gone through,
That I want you.
Alejandro: Florela, please…
Florela: In truth, my heart…
(I realize this now)
my heart belongs to another.
Alejandro: You can't possibly….
Florela: I do.
Alejandro: Florela…
Florela: It's over, Alejandro.
Laura. Will you have me?
Will you forgive me?

Duchess: Laura, is this the person you want to marry?

Laura: With all my heart.

Camacho: Well, this is turning out to be quite a day.

Paris: But…but…I won the game! I made it through the labyrinth. You can't do this to me. I deserve you, Laura. I deserve you.

Laura: I'm sorry, Paris.

Paris: Ma'am, if you'd be so kind…?

Duchess: Paris, I told you before, I won't go against my daughter's wishes.

Paris: Cruel and merciless, that's what you are. All of you. Defiant and cruel.

Camacho: Now, now, Paris…

Paris: Get off me.

Florela: *(to Camacho)* As for you, sir, I'm sure the Duchess will be happy to give you Finea.

Duchess: It'd be my pleasure.

Camacho: I'll take her. I've been eyeing her for a quite a while now.

Finea: That's not all you've been doing.

Duchess: Finea, give the Marquis your hand.

Camacho: Now, now, if truth be out, then let it be out, I'm no Marquis.
I'm a fine man, a humble man, but hardly nobility.

Finea: That's all right by me. I'll take you as I see you: honestly.

Camacho: Honest I'll be, my sweet,
for I'm done with wandering.
From Toledo to Mantua, from Mantua to Ferrara,
I've wandered as much as any man could.
I broke my ass, too, riding that bitch of a bicycle.

209

And I've not had a drop of pity
Or wine to comfort me,
Save for an embrace in the dark
By someone not fully known me at the time.
…
So, I'll take you, dear, if you'll take me.
And I promise you'll find me an enemy of hypocrisy.
When I love, my love is pure,
Even if I lose my way sometimes.
I beg your patience, that's all.
Marriage is not a simple thing.
Who are we? The answer is not easy.
There are so many strands to a story,
In passion, in ecstasy,
in the daily routines we call life,
There is always mystery.
It's beyond us,
Indeed, to our detriment,
To try to unravel everything.
…
As for sharing your life with me,
I'll admit I've my faults,
And no doubt, as time goes on,
there'll be the same curses and complaints,
the same pleasures craved,
and the same old stories told night after night
As we sit before the fire….
But isn't that what awaits us all
In this labyrinth of –
Infante: Excuse me? What about me?
Camacho: What about you? You've played your part.

Infante: And I've not even been recognized properly.
After all I've done.
Florela: What have you done?
Infante: I've done nothing but serve everyone
So they can tell their story.
Don't you recognize me? I'm Ricardo.
Alejandro & Florela: Ricardo?
Infante: And every selfless thing I've done,
As myself and the Infante of Aragon,
Has been out of love.
So, I ask you, what love is due me?
Estacio: My love.

Slight pause. Then Ricardo accepts Estacio's hand. They may even kiss.

Camacho: And so we continue
in our labyrinth of desire.

A moment. Then music fades up, perhaps Alison Moyet's 2004 vocal rendering of Purcell's "Dido's Lamet: when I am laid in earth."

Paris and Alejandro observe as the couples - Ricardo and Estacio, Camacho and Finea, Laura and Florela. – make their exit, paying their respects and bidding their farewell to the Duchess.

.

Paris and Alejandro remain, bereft.

END OF PLAY

THE MONSTER IN THE GARDEN

By Caridad Svich

Translated and adapted from the comedy
by Pedro Calderon de la Barca

Script History:

This translation/adaptation was made possible with the support of the Theatre Communications Group/PEW Charitable Trusts (US) National Theatre Artist Residency Program and INTAR Theatre, New York City.

Characters:

ACHILLES*
DEIDAMIA, princess
ULYSSES
LIDORO, nobleman, suitor of Deidamia
LIBIO and NYMPH 2, servant
DANTE and NYMPH 3
SIREN and NYMPH 1
THETIS, sea-goddess, Achilles' mother
THE KING
MUSICIANS (VO)

Setting:

On the island of Skiros.

Notes:

This play has only been performed twice, once in 1667
and once in 2000. Both productions were in Spain.
This adaptation/translation marks the first time this
'hidden play" of Calderon's has been rendered into
English.

*Achilles is preferably played by a woman, as was
done in the original and subsequent contemporary
production.

Author:

Pedro Calderon de la Barca (1600-1681) 's work dominated Spain's Golden Age of Theatre. His plays include *Life is a Dream*, *The Phantom Lady*, and *The Mayor of Zalamea*. Of his 120 surviving works, approximately 80 are *autos sacramentales*.

ACT ONE

Scene One

Dark. Sound of a storm on the ocean. A boat crashes.
Silence. Light comes up slowly upon an empty stretch of
sand. Libio is lying on the sand. Lidoro staggers about. He
approaches Libio, and checks to see if he is alive.

LIDORO: I am glad you're alive, my good man.
LIBIO: So am I!
LIDORO: For there is nothing here but wild plants
and the sound of birds grieving.
ACHILLES (VO): Oh woe is me! I am so melancholy!
LIDORO: Did you hear someone?
LIBIO: A lament from those rocks over there.
MUSICIANS (VO): *[sing]* Come, come, pilgrims, to
the divine temple of Mars.
LIDORO: Well, it is clear that this place is not
deserted, for there is not only weeping to be heard
but singing too.
LIBIO: Is there a place where people don't weep or
sing?
ACHILLES (VO): Oh woe is me! How melancholy!

Lidoro and Libio are interrupted by Dante.

DANTE: Heaven help me! Who is this I see?
LIDORO: Dante?!
DANTE: I kiss your feet, Lidoro.

217

LIDORO: In your arms I know I will have shelter,
Dante.
DANTE: Libio! You're here as well?
LIBIO: Your wonder cannot be too great!
DANTE: Whatever do you mean?
LIDORO: Tell me, dear Dante, what is this kingdom
of ash that I have come to?
DANTE: Before this island
was a mere desolate rock on shallow water,
A young prince named Peleus lived here.
This young prince was so taken with his desire for
Thetis, a glorious sea-nymph,
that he forced himself upon her.
Thetis was so offended by Peleus' actions,
that she destroyed their wedding bower
and set the island afire
until there was nothing was left.
Since that day it is said that in the caverns,
in the cavities between these rocks,
are heard the lamentations of human voices
torn by misery and anxiety.
LIDORO: In the heart of this mountain I see a temple.
DANTE: Mars' temple. King Lycomedes, Deidamia,
his daughter, and Ulysses are there
praying to the oracle.
LIDORO: Could this Deidamia be the same Deidamia,
Who stole my senses from afar,
and drove me to set sail at the worst possible hour
because I couldn't bear not to be at her side at once?
If this be true, if it is Deidamia, to whom I am already
betrothed, then fortune is mine!

DANTE: Indeed it is she; so you see, all you need do is come with me and we will speak to the King and she will be your wife.

LIDORO: No. I cannot. It is imprudent to stand before one's intended, one's beloved, in such a state as I am: wrecked and temporarily impoverished.

LIBIO: Right you are, for the poor are so disgusting that even seeming poor is cause for great alienation.

DANTE: So, what will you do, Lidoro?

LIDORO: Call me by another name. Let me wear a disguise. I will write to my father for his assistance and in due time, with riches restored, I will present myself to Deidamia with all the dignity she deserves.

DANTE: I will gladly embroider your lies.

Their conversation stops abruptly, as Ulysses exits the temple. The crowd awaits him.

ULYSSES:
No sooner did I enter the temple than Mars,
Than these words were heard:
"Troy will be destroyed
and burned to bits by the Greeks
if Achilles seeks his conquest
and lays Hector to rest.
Achilles, the wondrous human monster,
lives in these mountains."

Achilles' name echoes through the crowd.

KING: From Mars' sacred mouth we learn

that Achilles is among us.
He is here in these mountains and on his shoulders
rests the destruction of Troy.
Let us search far and wide for him.
Let us not cease in our seeking.
LIDORO: If a foreigner, dear sir,
A stranger to these parts, may speak…
I was tossed upon this shore, shipwrecked, and
ignorant of this land.
I saw nothing for a long time,
but I did hear human cries from within certain rocks.
KING: Thank you, kind man,
and lead me to this place
Because without doubt the wondrous being,
the monster Achilles,
Is hiding there.
DEIDAMIA: I should be the one to go.
KING: I will not allow it. It is rough terrain, daughter.
The soles of your feet will be ruined, Deidamia. I beg
you to stay here.
DEIDAMIA: How heavy it weighs on me to have to
obey you, father!
LIDORO: (Oh beautiful Deidamia! More beautiful
than in my dreams!)
ALL: To the ridge, to the summit, to the mountain.

They leave Deidamia, and Siren, her friend.

DEIDAMIA: Oh these skies are so unjust.
With such woes as I have
Why must they add their grief to mine?

SIREN: Why do you cry?
DEIDAMIA: How can you ask me such a question?
Have you forgotten that my father,
Tyrant of my desires,
Is trying to marry me off,
Knowing full well that I find men a great bore?
There has never been anyone
who has been worthy of my disdain.
How can I let a man call himself owner of my being?
How can I let a man behave
as if he were my conqueror
before ever giving me his affection?
SIREN: Unpleasant thoughts!
Best to put them out of your mind, than fear them.
Rest a while; I will sing to you.

Deidamia rests while Siren sings to her.

SIREN: Sad one,
Who cannot live a lie!
What does it matter
if you do not love me,
if when I listen to your deceitful affection,
I decide that I am happy?
…
I believe your face,
Although your face does lie,
Because I live for the very moment
When your affections are disguised.
…
Sad one,

Who cannot live a lie!

Deidamia sleeps.

The Siren's song makes Achilles, for the first time in his life, peer out of his cave. He cannot see the women from there. He hesitates, but cannot resist his own will. Achilles is like a feral child in aspect.

ACHILLES: What sweet voice wounds my ear?
What new bird is this that greets the sunrise today?
I have been ignorant of this sound my whole life.
I have lived my entire life locked up
in this crypt-like cave,
without ever seeing the pure light of day,
Without ever knowing what is the sky,
what are fields.
The deity who has raised me here
And who comes to see me at night,
Has ordered me to not go out during daylight,
And although I have been obedient thus far,
This unique song
forces me to break with her command.
I rise out of the grotto,
in hopes that it will perhaps sing again.
SIREN: *[sings]* If lies can disguise the love
that does not live in you,
What does it matter if there is harm in me?
I am ignorant of harm.
May I never be disillusioned,
Because it is better for me to live in delusion,

Than to die in desperation and jealousy.
Sad one,
Is one who does not live in illusion-wrapped!
ACHILLES: What a sweet voice! What a gentle voice!
Now that I have been able to break out of this prison
I must see what feathers this bird wears,
Because it has already stolen my soul.
SIREN: Sleep, sweet Deidamia. Rest.

Siren exits.

ACHILLES: The sun's pure light blinds me.
I am so eager to see the light of day
That I am faced with darkness.
Oh changeable light! How beauteous, how pleasing!
And if I can trust what I see,
I cannot see anything
that could be the bird whose sweet voice stirred me.
Oh how the imagination makes a pretense of things!
Oh how desire escapes reason!
That brilliant blue
Must be the sky
The earth, it seems to me,
Must be beautiful green;
This tree, this flower,
This bird, this clear fountain,
That ocean… Words lie;
Your voice has mistaken me.
Because there is only sky here, earth, ocean, tree,
Flower, bird and fountain.

He approaches Deidamia.

But oh, of everything I have seen so far
This is more real than anything else.
This is the best of them all.
The eye loves what it sees.
Oh God, if I dare touch it!
I am bold.
Oh, how I burn!
I turn to ice.
Oh treacherous snake!
To the eye you are made of snow
But to the touch you are made of fire.
And yet neither with your ice, nor with your ardor
Have you caused me harm;

I feel a small pain in my heart.
I have never had greater shame
Because my soul is full of pleasure;
I condemn myself for feeling thus,
While I delight in whatever might be its glory,
Gentle is this sentence which I am serving.
My soul binds itself to feel it again.
It seems to me
That yes, there are gods in this world,
There is royalty, and you must be it.
If you are not a god, then there are no gods,
For I know nothing else.

Siren returns.

SIREN: Fiery monster!
ACHILLES: Why do you call me thus?
SIREN: Go away. At once.
ACHILLES: Do I frighten you so? Listen, don't run.
Stay.
SIREN: If I stay here with you, I'm dead. May God
protect me!

*Siren screams. Her scream awakens Deidamia. Achilles is
now between them.*

DEIDAMIA: What is this? What voices do I hear?
Moreover, dear heavens, what is this that I see?
ACHILLES: Do not be frightened by what you see.
DEIDAMIA: (A living statue; I am made of ice)
ACHILLES: I only wish to know
Within the confusion and doubts
In which I seem to live,
If it was necessary
For that other goddess to die
So that you could live.
When you were lying there life-less
How is it that now you are with life before me?
When you were once only an icy statue
Now, you breathe.
Tell me how can this be?
How could you make it live?
You are even more beautiful than it.
And tell me, if I were to walk alongside you
Could I embrace your soul,
And thus forever be with you?

DEIDAMIA: Your wild aspect turns fear to horror.
Your reasoning is not rational
Even if your voice speaks reason.
My quick mind
Dares to judge, and not in vain,
That you are a man, a human being.
ACHILLES: Your soul imagines like a tyrant.
I think of you as divine
And you think of me as mortal!
I am the son of a goddess.
This I know about myself.
Since the day I was born
I have known nothing else.
DEIDAMIA: How do you mean?
ACHILLES: It is cruel of you to ask me.

Siren stirs.

DEIDAMIA: My siren is waking.
ACHILLES: How did she resurrect herself thus,
without being lost to you and this world?
Have you life and soul?
SIREN: Yes.
ACHILLES: So they were yours to begin with?
DEIDAMIA: No.
ACHILLES: What a great author
must be he who can give each body
A soul and each life a human shape.
Who are you?
SIREN: A woman.

ACHILLES: Such a sweet word. Woman. And you,
what are you?
DEIDAMIA: A woman.
ACHILLES: What tender pleasures,
What beautiful ones.
God indeed must be alive to have made such
beautiful animals as woman.
Moreover, if my eyesight doesn't fail me
Although you are both unparalleled
There is a great difference between you;
For if I look at both of you
with equal degrees of affection
I can see quite clearly that one of you has a more
beautiful soul than the other.
You have a soul, and yet somehow you give it to me,
And yet you can still keep it inside you.
What greater power did the heavens give you?
Because to look at you is enough for me
And yet to look at you is not enough.
Your beauty delights me.
It gives me passion
And with mutual admiration
With conflicting desires
You remain in my eyes
And go straight into my heart.
SIREN: Mister monster, there is, I must confess
Much to say about what is going to happen;
But I'm not up for it.
DEIDAMIA: I am exhausted.
I cannot think from seeing so much wild beauty
In such an uncivilized being.

SIREN: *(exiting)* Run away, madam.

DEIDAMIA: I cannot move. Fear has shackled me.

ACHILLES: Why does she flee from me thus?

From just looking at me?

Although if I speak true,

I would not be so alone

If you offered me your company.

DEIDAMIA: No, no do not draw near. Go another way.

ACHILLES: Do not run from me. Stay. Wait.

DEIDAMIA: Let go of me.

ACHILLES: I will not, until I know

Who gives me life and death.

SIREN'S (VO): Quick! Deidamia is in the arms of a monster.

ACHILLES: What are these voices I hear?

DEIDAMIA: My people. They will kill you.

ACHILLES: It is in vain to fight the great Achilles.

DEIDAMIA: What did you say? You are Achilles?

ACHILLES: This much I do know.

He is about to exit but Deidamia stops him.

DEIDAMIA: I will detain you now.

ACHILLES: What good will it do you?

DEIDAMIA: Is there no one who can hear me?

Lidoro arrives, sword in hand.

LIDORO: Fiery monster!

Deidamia embraces Lidoro to stop the fight.

DEIDAMIA: Don't kill him, this is Achilles.

LIDORO: What did you say?

ACHILLES: What rage arises in my chest
To see her embrace him?!
I almost hate her now,
When before I loved her.

LIDORO: *[To Deidamia]* I do not fear his visage,
But your words stop me. I will not kill him.

ACHILLES: Do not hold him thus. Break away now.
(Let's see if he who kills with words can kill with
arms)

LIDORO: Are you Achilles?

ACHILLES: I am.

LIDORO: The sacred deities have decreed you to be
the one who will give Greece vengeance from Troy. I
want to be your friend.

ACHILLES: Well, I do not wish to be yours.
It is infamy to be a friend with your tongue
And an enemy with your soul.

LIDORO: Why "enemy?"

ACHILLES: I don't know.

LIDORO: What reason have I given you to feel thus?

ACHILLES: I know the reason even if I cannot name
it.

DEIDAMIA: Well, it's my luck to capture you, and so
the quarrel must stop. Come with me.

ACHILLES: That is not possible.

DEIDAMIA: Why not?

ACHILLES: Because the deity whom I live for will miss me when she discovers I am not in the prison from which I have broken from. I do not doubt that her vengeance will make my life unhappy. And thus, despite my desires… Goodbye, governing deity.
LIDORO: Wait.
ACHILLES: It is not possible.

Achilles flees. Lidoro goes after Achilles.

DEIDAMIA: The wind itself
must have given him wings.
How quickly he disappears into the mountain.

King, Ulysses, Dante and Libio enter.

KING: Beautiful Deidamia, what has happened?
DEIDAMIA: Those that look for fortune do not find it.
And those that don't, do.
I was not looking for Achilles
And yet I found him.
ULYSSES: Where is he?
DEIDAMIA: You will find him if you follow his footprints.
ULYSSES: Guide us. We will follow your divine light.

All follow Deidamia, except for Libio.

LIBIO: Let the brave ones go.
I was never fond of chasing monsters.
I have enough with chasing pigeons and rabbits.

Because when a man
Tires of hunting
At day's end all he can get for
His catch is four measly pennies
In the town square.

Achilles falls upon the rocks before Libio.

ACHILLES: Am I not one of you?
Why am I being chased?
Am I being punished
for stepping out into the light of day
To seek out a voice that stole my dreams?
Moreover, oh heavens, in midst of all this confusion
I have lost my way back to the grotto.
Where will I go to find it?
LIBIO: Not where I go. *(hides)*
DEIDAMIA (VO): He leapt from those high crags.
LIDORO: Take the mountain.
DANTE: To the beach.
ULYSSES: To the harbor.
KING: To the rocks.
ACHILLES: Since everyone is after me, I will hide
here.

He hides where Libio hid.

LIBIO: Is this the only place you could hide?
ACHILLES: Who is there?
LIBIO: A wolf who fell into a trap.
ACHILLES: Who are you?

LIBIO: I'll go find out. Be right back.

ACHILLES: Why do you flee?

LIBIO: From nothing. Only you.

ACHILLES: Why?

LIBIO: Because I wish to flee.

ACHILLES: Now I understand there is a great
difference among men,
Because there are those who fear me
And there are those that cause rage in me.
Come here.

LIBIO: I'm fine right here.

ACHILLES: Have you seen on this mountain the
mouth of a cave covered with brambles?

LIBIO: No, but you go on ahead. It's over there.

ACHILLES: You go first. So you may guide me.

LIBIO: I can guide you from here.

ACHILLES: Draw near.
What is the name of the sweet nightmare
that is both icy with time
And can burn your heart completely?

LIBIO: What have you seen?

ACHILLES: A woman.

LIBIO: If I'm not mistaken, this is love.

ACHILLES: Then after I saw her,
I felt an even stronger passion,
cousin of the previous one yet opposite in feeling.
What is it called?

LIBIO: What did you see?

ACHILLES: She embraced another man.

LIBIO: Well, that's called jealousy.

ACHILLES: Jealousy? You lie.

Jealousy cannot be,
For someone so close to heaven
And so far from hell.
What cure is there for this?
LIBIO: Forget her.
ACHILLES: Give me some of your forgetfulness.
LIBIO: I left it at home.
But if you wait for me a bit
I'll go look for it and I'll come back in a rickshaw
filled with oblivion.
ACHILLES: What's keeping you, then? Run.
LIBIO: I'll come back in an instant. *(leaves)*
DEIDAMIA (VO): The branches rustle. Surround the
area.

Achilles tries to hide. Lidoro stops Achilles.

LIDORO: Stop, you prodigious human beast,
mine will be the joy
Of bringing you to Deidamia's feet.
ACHILLES: You aren't lucky enough to please her.
I leave without fear.

Ulysses stops him.

ULYSSES: Stop now, reasonable human monster
For my hope is
The heavens grant me the fortune to
bring you to Mars' altar.

Dante stops him.

DANTE: Wait, prodigious one of these mountains.
Mine is the victory.
ACHILLES: Where can I go surrounded as I am like
this?

King stops him.

KING: Surrender now.

Deidamia stops him.

DEIDAMIA: Don't go.
Know you did not offend me.
It is no shame to be sought
By those who would honor you.
ACHILLES: I don't know anything about that.
All I know is: the deity who keeps me will be angry
If she doesn't find me where she left me.
ALL: How are you going to escape us all?
ACHILLES: Divine deity
How is it I am out of your love
Because of so small an infraction?

*The mountain opens. Thetis appears. She embraces Achilles
and carries him as if he were a child into the bosom of the
mountain. The mountain closes. Silence.*

DEIDAMIA: The center of the earth
Tears open her hard breasts
In order to hide him.
Who can doubt that a powerful deity

Watches over him?
KING: Against such a powerful deity
Human power is not enough.

They exit. Ulysses remains.

ULYSSES: Although they all flee
I will remain;
On the opposite path
I will find him, powerful deity,
wherever you may keep him.

Scene Two

Inside the cave.

ACHILLES: Is this mercy?
THETIS: Yes.
ACHILLES: Well, I don't want it.
THETIS: What are you thinking of doing?
ACHILLES: I am going to throw myself,
Desperate in my resolve,
off the highest cliff
and straight into the sea.
Where my life
Will finally end, and my anxieties will finally be over.
THETIS: Think now.
ACHILLES: It is in vain.
THETIS: Consider…
ACHILLES: It's not possible…
THETIS: Look…

ACHILLES: What should I look at?
What advice should I heed?
What should I consider
When I am subject to such a tyrannical force,
that for a second time
Seeks to reduce me
To an even narrower prison
Than the one I was tossed
Into my young years?
Well, no, it is too late to be obedient.
Before I saw the sun's rays
Before I saw the harmony of the skies
The pride of the mountains
The splendor of the flowers
The beauty of the birds
And the restless, majestic sea
I tolerated my destiny
with blind, faithful ignorance,
and eternal patience.
But after I saw them
And after I saw that Deidamia
was the most beautiful of all of nature's wonders,
How can you expect me
To live my life without her,
and without the beauty of the world?
Cruel merciful one,
You guard and watch over me
you raised me and have tended to me
you praise me and torment me.
But forgive me, with all due respect,
although I wish to obey you

My passion does not allow me to obey you.
I must follow Deidamia.
She is my light.
Although the gods may not wish it,
And you may take my life.
THETIS: This cruelty, which you so name,
Has safeguarded you from a sorry fate.
ACHILLES: Can there be a crueler destiny than one
that robs me of my life?
And since life's fiery constellation
Has destined me to two deaths,
At least let me lose my life
The way I choose to do so,
If I am indeed to lose it.
Come back to me, beautiful Deidamia
And all those who follow you too!
Achilles is calling you. Achilles!
THETIS: Lower your voice. Think what you say…
ACHILLES: I have already told you
it is in vain to do so.
It is unclear to me why you are obliged
To hide who I am (and who you are).
But this I know: as long as I cannot return
To see the sky where this deity lives -
She who has made it impossible
For my anxieties to find solace -
I will not be ready-tamed
To the yoke of your obedience.
THETIS: Such beauty drags you?
ACHILLES: Such that I have no choice but to follow
it.

THETIS: There's no forgetting it?
ACHILLES: I cannot.
THETIS: There's no sanity?
ACHILLES: None left me.
THETIS: No free will?
ACHILLES: My will is not my own.
THETIS: No freedom?
ACHILLES: It is alien to me.
THETIS: No remedy?
ACHILLES: None. I will die unless I see Deidamia
again.
THETIS: Well, since your passion
has reached such an extreme,
Let mine reach one as well,
And may one shock
Be small repair for such unhappiness.
ACHILLES: What do you intend?
THETIS: That you know the danger you're in,
And for me to serve as liaison
So that you may be near Deidamia
And yet remain safe with me.
ACHILLES: What are you waiting for?
THETIS: I fear it won't seem probable.
ACHILLES: All is easy in love.
THETIS: But if it is frightful?
ACHILLES: I have no fear.
THETIS: But if it is terrifying?
ACHILLES: What of it?
THETIS: If it is strange?
ACHILLES: Let it be so.
THETIS: And if…?

ACHILLES: Say it.
THETIS: It occurs as if it were out of a page of fiction?
ACHILLES: My life is already myth.
What of it if it seems a fiction?
THETIS: ...I am, wondrous Achilles
for now I must reveal myself,
Thetis, daughter of Neptune,
The first god of the spheres.
With other sea nymphs
I roamed the ridge of this mountain
Crowned with pearls both natural and unnatural.
Peleus, proud prince, enamored of my beauty
Solicited my affection;
And although it was impossible to desire it,
Against my resistance he decided...
It is enough for you to know
That you are the product of a violent encounter,
So do not blame me for your fate
But instead the star under which you were born;
For you are so unfortunate
That while most people
Pride themselves of being born out of love
You were born out of force.
After which I gave Peleus his death
And I set fire to this island,
leaving not a trace untouched.
In this horror, in this fright,
In this wonder,
Something struggled within my breast
Upon seeing you:
A rancor mixed with tenderness.

What innocence from such malice.
I raised you in secret
Within these rocks;
You grew up on wild fruits and leaves.
Seeing your prodigious birth
I wished throughout your life
To read your destiny in the golden letters
of that book which is the sky.
And I managed to find out that a fiery battle
would threaten you in the future,
A battle most bloody.
I also wished adding reason to reason,
and force to force
That you would not see this world.
But woe to anyone
who tries to fight the will of the gods!
Mars, in his oracle,
orders that in the center of those ruins
You will be found
because you alone are needed for this war.
When you are consumed by so blind a passion
to ask you not to live is to ask you to die.
How Achilles, can you conquer love,
the oracle and the gods?

Pause.

Deidamia's cousin was called Astrea.
Her ship was lost at sea.
No one in this island knows her.
If you wear her dress and her name,

You will be safe from harm.
Disguised, let us see what
Power the heavens have over your destiny.
ACHILLES: If I am to live with Deidamia
If I am to adore her beauty
What matters if I lose my name,
my self, my honor and my fame?
Do not delay this happiness you offer me;
I am persuaded.
The hours will seem like centuries
until this is done.
THETIS: If this be true, then to the sea!

ACT TWO

Scene One

Achilles is transformed in the ocean. Prelude to the masque.

THETIS: Beautiful nymphs of mine!
NYMPH 1: What do you wish?
NYMPH 2: What do you desire?
NYMPH 3: What do you say?
What do you demand?
ALL NYMPHS: We are always at your service, Thetis.
THETIS: I wish for you to take this rough diamond
And with the most sumptuous jewels and fabrics
That live in the archives of the sea
Polish him in such a manner that
From horror he goes to beauty.
So disguise his shape

That he who was once monster of this wilderness
Become a monster in a garden.

Nymphs sing. A masque play.

NYMPH 2: In good time let it be
In good time
NYMPH 3: Change his form
From horror to beauty
NYMPH 1: Let the monster of this wilderness
Become…
In time now.
In good time.
NYMPH 1: Come where your nymphs
NYMPH 2: Attend to your desire
NYMPH 3: Labor over your beauty
And polish your form.
NYMPH 1: Fortunate are we
NYMPH 2: You yourself have said
NYMPH 3: To change your face
As much as your shape
NYMPH 2: From horror to beauty.
So that you be…
NYMPH 1: In time now
ALL NYMPHS: In good time.
ACHILLES: Made of ambient skin,
I am made a mosaic of halves
Unrecognizable to myself.
I pretend I am not made a stranger to this body.
Here are soft breasts on a hard torso,
A stirring womb, and slim hips.

A moon-lit mirror finds me in watery shape.
I dare catch sight of my fragmented self
in this fluid glass:
NYMPH 2: From horror to beauty.
NYMPH 3: So that you be…
ALL NYMPHS: In time now
NYMPH 1: In time…
ACHILLES: Sky, sun, stars, moon,
Beasts, birds, fish, brutes,
Since perforce my life seems a myth
Give me ingenuity to disguise my ignorance.
Let the monster of the wilderness
Become the monster in the garden.

Scene Two

Outside the cave.

ULYSSES: What new oracle is this
that rings in the air?
Without Achilles this war
Will never resolve itself in our favor.
This is what Mars' oracle has decreed.
How can the gods give us this news,
But not reveal where he is?
An enemy power is allowing Achilles to escape us.
But I will not surrender to these obstacles.
If there is a god who keeps him
There are others who can seek him out.
These days and nights
My cunning has come up with two instruments:

One of cured rough skins
And the other of smooth twisted metals;
Both resound with the kind of luck
That harmoniously enjoins the sounds of war,
And calls up the voice of Mars
and the language of the winds
And stirs up the soul of the soldier.
I will find Achilles yet.

Scene Three

Lidoro, Dante and Libio, hidden, wait for Deidamia to appear in the garden.

LIDORO: Observe carefully now
If her visage
Carries in it any sign at all
In favor of my inconstant fortune.
DANTE: She draws near, so it is wise that you play my servant now.

Deidamia with Siren in the garden

DEIDAMIA: Who, Siren, do you see here?
SIREN: Your future husband's ambassador.
DEIDAMIA: What's new, ambassador?
DANTE: Much to fear, madam.
A letter from the King of Epirus has arrived:
"Lidoro, obedient of his free will, has shipped out
Because he wished that no one else but him came for you."

LIDORO: *(aside)* Is she happy to hear this?

LIBIO: *(aside)* No.

DANTE: And since the letter has arrived without him
I am saddened
Moreover because a ship was found wrecked ashore,
Such was told to me by that traveler over there.

LIDORO: And now? Is she happy?

LIBIO: Yes.

LIDORO: You lie. At first she was happy,
Now with this news she must be sad.

LIBIO: I know little of feelings
But I saw neither one or the other.

DEIDAMIA: I am sad to hear, sir that what you say
may be true.

LIDORO: You see? She does care about me.

LIBIO: Fine.

DEIDAMIA: Tell that traveler there to speak to me
Because I would like to know what happened.
Weren't you to the first one to come to my aid
when my fear forced me to believe Achilles was that
fierce monster?

LIDORO: I was indeed, dear lady
Who presumed nothing would make me happier
Than to sacrifice my life for yours –
And now you find me humbly at your feet.

DEIDAMIA: I confess I remain grateful to you and
empathize with your sad state
Knowing you have been shipwrecked.
And to ease this state in which you find yourself
rest your eyes on me.

From this moment on: I offer to make possible
whatever you desire.

LIDORO: I kiss the ground you walk on
If such earth as this I am worthy enough to kiss;
And since you give so freely
I will tell you my desire.

DEIDAMIA: Tell me.

LIDORO: Not now.

DEIDAMIA: Why not?

LIDORO: Because I don't dare…

DEIDAMIA: What?

LIDORO: I should think first before I say anything.

DEIDAMIA: Well, when you have thought about it,
return to me.

LIDORO: How is it that knowing of my fate at sea
You have not asked about Lidoro's as well?

DEIDAMIA: I don't know.
It's either true or false.
If not true, what need have I to feel anything
And if it is true, what could I do to change things?
Was the lost ship from Acaya?
Because what does indeed trouble me much is if my
cousin Astrea was on that ship.

LIDORO: The ship was from Epirus. And Lidoro was
on it.

DEIDAMIA: Since it wasn't Astrea's ship
That means she was not in harm's way.
Give me your report later, then.

She leaves with Siren.

LIDORO: Deidamia doesn't seem too interested in our marriage.

DANTE: What will you do?

LIDORO: To write, my dear Dante,
A report of such breadth
That not knowing who I am
She will want to know who I am,
Because I am inspired by the muse today:
"Great acts of honor are herein narrated.
No one but me
have the gods held in such esteem."

Scene Four

King and Ulysses enter.

ULYSSES: Tell me what you want me to tell the princes of Greece.

KING: My friendship appreciates
Entering into this heroic alliance.
But until I see Achilles sail off to Troy
(and we all saw him
even though we do not know
the god who hides him from us)
I will not dare to go to battle
Because it will be a losing one;
Mars makes it difficult for us.

ULYSSES: I will tell them this on both our behalves.
And I swear from this day on that I will bring Achilles to you.

Disguised Achilles enters with Thetis.

ACHILLES: No sooner did I see the palace so grand
but all my senses were disturbed.
THETIS: Well, get a hold of yourself.
Try to mask your feelings. Recover quickly.
ACHILLES: Your Majesty, sir... I... if...when...
Astrea asks to speak with you.
KING: Beautiful Astrea, your confusion excuses you
from fluent rhetoric. You must kiss Deidamia's hand.

Deidamia arrives accompanied by Siren.

ACHILLES: Beautiful Deidamia,
The heavens are mere shadows to your radiant light.
Please let me kiss your hand
And forgive me for not coming here sooner;
We have so much to tell each other
And yet I cannot remember anything
since last I saw you.
Only you remain in my mind.
To touch your hand
is something one can never forget.
DEIDAMIA: (Never in my life
have I seen such beauty!)
Rise, sweet cousin, and believe me
When I say that I wish for you
Not to be my servant but my friend;
There are many ways to value –
And my arms attest to this –
The treasure of your kinship.

ACHILLES: (Oh, what good fortune is this
when much is ventured
and so much is gained.
I am in Deidamia's arms.
If anyone blames my disguise,
Let them see how many they wear
to please their lover.)
KING: Now Ulysses,
since this occasion and its obligations,
Interrupted our conversation,
let us return to matters at hand.
Not once but a thousand times
Do I give my word to the highest powers
That on the day Achilles is found again,
I will give all my support to help Greece
so that she may defeat Troy.
ACHILLES: (Dear heavens!
Is it so important that I obey the will of the gods?)
ULYSSES: And I say again that I give my word
Once and a thousand times over,
To not rest until I find Achilles.

*Dante and Libio enter. Libio speaks to Lidoro while Dante
speaks to the King.*

DANTE: Near us, sir, is a ship,
That dipped rapidly through the waves
And found its nest in our port.
In that ship I saw
Without a doubt, Lidoro, as his letter said.
His flag assures me.

KING: If it is Lidoro who has reached our shores
There will be quite a recompense for you.
(a treasure chest is in that ship)
DEIDAMIA: (There is no recompense for me.
Only tears.
For I am a woman without a proper dowry.)
DANTE: (When the King is happy
she grows sad and dismayed)
KING: Let's go to the dock
So that I may see that snowy swan
Swim on the sea-foam.
Goodbye, Deidamia.

Ulysses and Dante exit.

DEIDAMIA: May the heavens watch over you!
(to Siren) Let us go to the garden and entertain
ourselves with some music. Come on, Astrea.

She leaves with Siren. Achilles follows but is stopped by Thetis.

THETIS: Before you leave, listen to me.
You have heard how sought after you are.
ACHILLES: Yes.
THETIS: Then I don't have to tell you that in keeping
your identity hidden lies your safety.
Fate is in your hands, Achilles.
Be silent and restrained
Because you have little time
Before your time is up.

ACHILLES: That is something
you should tell my love.
It is not possible for fire to suffer silently
Without some smoke, if not sparks.

Thetis and Nymphs leave.

Scene Five

Deidamia with a telescope looks at the sea.

DEIDAMIA: Oh, proud ship
Who comes through the crystal waves
If you are the owner of my cruel shame
Do not reach the shore!
For what you do is against me.
I was not born to love,
Despite how many times you draw near.
Why, sailor, don't you go to another port!

Sees Achilles.

You're here, Astrea?

ACHILLES: I did not wish to hear you.
DEIDAMIA: Little do I care that you did.
Oh, Astrea, it was you who heard me.
To entreat your love
I can assure you
For you to hear me is not a burden.
I confide in you. I trust you.

But you must know why
I must be careful of what I say!
Truth be told,
although it seems so soon, I am fond of you.
ACHILLES: I kiss your hand not out of duty
but for the pleasure of kissing it.
DEIDAMIA: Against my will, my father the King
arranged my marriage to Lidoro, Prince of Epirus.
ACHILLES: You are married?
DEIDAMIA: No.
ACHILLES: Then my heart has hope.
DEIDAMIA: But we have made arrangements…
ACHILLES: Well then if you're not married, then why
such sorrow?
DEIDAMIA: Listen.
ACHILLES: Tell me.
DEIDAMIA: So much was I against
surrendering my liberty
To one I did not know
That what was once merely unavoidable
Has now become hateful.
If my father married me to a man I could see
And this man suffered my disdain with rare dignity,
he would win my affection today,
and tomorrow even more.
A discreetly gallant and noble love
would have an effect on me.
But to ask me to love someone
whom I don't even know is fierce slavery.
How could I not feel otherwise burdened?
ACHILLES: I take it you mean

that if you know that someone loved you
And that he suffered your indifference
You would be less disgusted by his desire?
DEIDAMIA: Who is indifferent?
To love me well is not offensive to me.
ACHILLES: May the heavens give you life.
DEIDAMIA: What do you care about all this, Astrea?
Speak, or else beware my punishment
Otherwise you would speak.
ACHILLES: I am obliged if I say what I know
I won't know what I say.
DEIDAMIA: Well I want to know.
ACHILLES: And I wish to say it.
DEIDAMIA: Say it then.
ACHILLES: (This may be easier than I thought!
The habit of speaking
Comes from this woman's habit)
Most beautiful Deidamia,
Your happy perfection
Gives May its order
And gives April its laws:
On the grand isle of Mars
A young man saw you
Prefer the red of the carnation
to the white of the jasmine.
He saw you
but he could not declare his love for you
Because all he knew
Was to feel… blindly.
Your absence and his feeling
Have forced him to come to your court disguised;

Love is a civil war
In which all tricks are fair.
His blood is noble.
So much so that he can compete
with the most sacred
Lineage of any church.
That masked man
You know as I:
His name I cannot tell you.
(This is the one secret I must keep from you
so as not to outrage you upon hearing my name:
Achilles)
DEIDAMIA: I appreciate your warning.
It will spare me embarrassment, I'm sure.
I beg of you, Astrea,
I order you to tell me
who this man is as soon as you see him.
If you do not, I will complain about you.
ACHILLES: (Love, you dare much)
DEIDAMIA: Why did you stop? Tell me.
ACHILLES: You can see him from here.
DEIDAMIA: I see no one.
ACHILLES: Look closely, you will see.
DEIDAMIA: In the whole garden there is no one but
us two girls.
ACHILLES: Only us girls?
DEIDAMIA: Yes.
ACHILLES: Well, if you say we are alone
And I who am here am your lover
The riddle is easily solved.
DEIDAMIA: What?

ACHILLES: Your lover is here.

Lidoro, dressed like a prince, enters with a letter in hand.

DEIDAMIA: (What do I see?)
ACHILLES: (Woe is me.)
LIDORO: This report, madam, will let you know who I am.

Deidamia tears the letter.

DEIDAMIA: This is how I treat letters given to me
By someone who dares enter my garden…
LIDORO: (What do I hear!)
DEIDAMIA: And shows up in disguise...
ACHILLES: (She thinks I meant him!)
LIDORO: (Someone recognized me, and told her who I was)
DEIDAMIA: No need of that here.
LIDORO: Woe is me.
DEIDMAIA: I know who you are.
LIDORO: Well then if you know, hear me out.
ACHILLES: (Look how sad she has become)
DEIDAMIA: (Heart, how you must suffer.)
LIDORO: Defeated by the sea
I landed on this isle of Mars
Where I saw your beauty.
DEIDAMIA: That's what you say.
ACHILLES: Yes…
(I have come to be the third wheel against myself;
for I declared myself on behalf of another)

LIDORO: Seeing as I was so unhappy
I hid my name and identity.
To come to you as I am
To feign my name should not cause offense…
DEIDAMIA: What do you mean "to come as you are?"
LIDORO: You do say you know who I am, yes?
DEIDAMIA: Well, now I don't want to know
Since I know full well;
And so, if you know who you are,
Tell my father.
LIDORO: If I…
DEIDAMIA: No more.
LIDORO: Could…
DEIDAMIA: Enough.
LIDORO: Judge…
DEIDAMIA: Not a word from your lips.
LIDORO: It will go, to give us time.
DEIDAMIA: For what?
LIDORO: To realize
That my crime is so noble
That I only err against myself.
I do not dare seem
Because I do not dare show off. *(exits)*
DEIDAMIA: Astrea, do not follow me.
ACHILLES: Have I offended?
DEIDAMIA: Yes.
ACHILLES: In saying who it was?
DEIDAMIA: No.
ACHILLES: Then how?
DEIDAMIA: In not telling me.

Could there be a more treacherous act?
Could there be a more vile action
That three times removed from love
To speak to me that there is a lover disguised for me
And to find out it was Lidoro?
ACHILLES: I don't know.
DEIDAMIA: You lie to me again.
ACHILLES: Do not insult me;
I saw you were upset.
Perhaps, since things were hopeless
I dared to see you.
DEIDAMIA: What?
ACHILLES: I did not mean him.
DEIDAMIA: Then whom?
ACHILLES: Me.
Let honor return to this cipher,
The enigma of this palace,
who was after you always.
You see and do not see,
You speak to him and do not speak;
You hear and do not hear
Because it is the delirium
Of the gods,
Of love's frenzy.
A prodigious monster is hidden in your garden.

ACT THREE

Scene One

Deidamia in the room with the Siren.

SIREN: In the sun's burnished glow.

The soft lights shine with such exquisite splendor

That they compete with the stars.

DEIDAMIA: How you sing, my siren. Such sweet music. Tell me, has Astrea come by?

SIREN: She is on her way.

Enter Achilles dressed as Astrea.

DEIDAMIA: Dearest Astrea, where have you been? I have missed you.

Why are you so sad, cousin?

ACHILLES: As I was walking over here I heard…

DEIDAMIA: What?

ACHILLES: That a message is being sent to you.

DEIDAMIA: A message from whom?

ACHILLES: Lidoro…

DEIDAMIA: You start badly.

ACHILLES: Upon knowing a merchant

from a nearby island had arrived,

Lidoro has sent him to you so that you may choose whatever jewels you wish.

DEIDAMIA: Such generosity augers either malice or ignorance.

ACHILLES: You will send him away, then?

DEIDAMIA: I don't know how I should respond.

If I respond with cruelty or disdain

He'll take it somehow the wrong way,

And if I don't, I'll make you angry.

ACHILLES: Well, since you're so full of doubts

I will tell him to enter.

Enter Ulysses and Libio disguised as merchants.

LIBIO: My back is undone
From this portable store I am carrying.
ULYSSES: The great prince Lidoro
Who confides in my counsel
sends you a great treasure:
Something you may bargain for.
DEIDAMIA: Let's see what jewels you bring.
ULYSSES: (I'll take notice of everything.)
DEIDAMIA: I don't want anything for myself
But for my friends I would be happy to bargain for.
ULYSSES: Take out those silks and unfold them.
LIBIO: What color would you like? What's your
pleasure?
DEIDAMIA: I don't know.
ULYSSES: Take out the jewels.
LIBIO: What do you think of this diamond Cupid?
DEIDAMIA: Foolish is he who finds in it love
The more perfect something seems,
The less it will deliver.
SIREN: Well, leaving philosophy aside,
I have not seen a more beautiful jewel.
I think it is rich and in good taste.
LIBIO: It is rich.
DEIDAMIA: Well, then, my siren, it is yours.
LIBIO: This crown should please you.
DEIDAMIA: What do you say, friend?
ACHILLES: I don't like it.
DEIDAMIA: Why not?
ACHILLES: Because it is in your hand

259

and not in mine.

LIBIO: It is a royal eagle.

The sun has turned its feathers golden.

DEIDAMIA: Do you like this one?

ACHILLES: No. Its flights have not been promising.

LIBIO: A ruby snake, then.

DEIDAMIA: Do you like this one?

ACHILLES: I will say no to everything.

DEIDAMIA: You'll upset me

if you don't choose something.

ACHILLES: Do you want it?

DEIDAMIA: I do.

ACHILLES: Well then I'll take this shield, this spear,

these feathers and this sword.

DEIDAMIA: That's what you have chosen?

ACHILLES: Yes.

DEIDAMIA: To what end?

ACHILLES: Perhaps we'll have need of them at night.

ULYSSES: Strange preference. Where there are jewels,

you take weapons.

ACHILLES: Yes because even among women,

there are those that are not.

DEIDAMIA: How foolish you are.

(to Ulysses) Do not tell Lidoro any of this.

I am grateful for his attentions, and his generosity,

and do not doubt his kindness toward me;

in his name let him know

I take these ribbons for myself.

ACHILLES: And I this shield.

ULYSSES: I will tell him everything you wish.

LIBIO: And if you don't mind

I'll come back another day
Because maybe you will find
something to your liking, then.
DEIDAMIA:Come back whenever you wish.
What think you of this, Siren?
SIREN: There is much to say
Because let us not talk of it now
A day of gifts is not one to complain about.

Scene Two

*Night. Achilles and Deidamia are in the garden. Achilles is
dressed as a man. Each one thinks they are alone.*

ACHILLES: Pale threatening sky on a cold night,
your feeble shadow
Fades and astonishes
The sun's light, the blush of dawn;
Astonishment brings as much surprise as horror,
all fear, all fright.
DEIDAMIA: All fear, all fright, all horror.
As soon as I step on the ground
I glimpse
In the wrinkles of the night's mantle,
So attentive to my lament,
Not a light, not a reflection, not a star.
ACHILLES: Not a light, not a reflection, not a star
In the sky is seen.
Oh how much it favors my disguise,
And beautiful Deidamia!
When in this costume I come to speak to her

261

The sun is gone, the moon flees,
the wind stops!
DEIDAMIA: The sun is gone, the moon flees,
the wind stops.
Firm and constant I come to see a lover;
So enigmatic is love
that there is no point to deciphering it.
It moves, it marvels, it arises.
ACHILLES: It moves, it marvels, it arises.
Such is my life's adoration.
Deidamia is she.
She greets the flowers, the leaves and the stems
Like a new dawn discovering a new fragrance.
DEIDAMIA: From the leaves, the stems,
and the flowers
Breathed by all
Caution stirs
the guardian of love.
ACHILLES: My owner, my sovereign!
DEIDAMIA: Dear heavens!
ACHILLES: The sun has risen.
DEIDAMIA: The dawn has arrived.
ACHILLES & DEIDAMIA: The day has come.
DEIDAMIA: The trees, the flowers and the fountains
Seeing that the night had come
And you were detained
Accused you of lateness.
ACHILLES: Beautiful goddess of snow,
it is not so strange
That the sun fears to see you today.
DEIDAMIA: Why?

ACHILLES: He who dies of jealousy
will see it everywhere.
DEIDAMIA: Say what you mean.
ACHILLES: Do you like that I have come here to the
garden at night dressed in this costume?
DEIDAMIA: Yes, because in woman's clothes it seems
to me your affection would be much more violent.
ACHILLES: Then I am twice a monster.
Your woman by day, your man by night;
You do not deserve either my love
As woman or man;
Because you do not appeal to me
As either woman or man.
DEIDAMIA: Please do not say such things.
What more do you want from me
That knowing who you are,
I continue to hide you?
What more do you want?
To my sorrows
You owe your happiness;
I have feigned illness to delay my marriage
ACHILLES: Do not be angry,
although you have reason to be.
What does it matter to say "oh I am love's sovereign"
If my gentilities serve to aggravate your sorrow?
Look what it has done to me to favor you.
In order to protect my life
I have killed myself.
DEIDAMIA: Could I be someone I am not?
ACHILLES: Do you cry?
DEIDAMIA: No. I only wish to cry with tears

Like someone with a proud rebellious heart.

Musicians are heard.

MUSICIANS (VO): Fugitive eyes
Over the garden wall.
ACHILLES: What voices do I hear?
DEIDAMIA: Do not be frightened, do not be upset,
They are Lidoro's musicians
They think their songs
will distract me from my sadness.
ACHILLES: I hope you do not mean to offend me.
MUSICIANS (VO): Moisten their eyelashes
Upon the jasmines and carnations
DEIDAMIA: May he sing while I cry!
He declares his love and it is my oblivion.
ACHILLES: Can someone who feels so much
not feel anything?
MUSICIANS (VO): Their smiling tears
Recount joyful grievances
Between the bars of a song,
And the murmurs of the ocean current.

Achilles, sword in hand, wishes to go toward the music.
Deidamia stops him]

ACHILLES: Let my sword make them weep,
It is not right that you suffer, and they sing.

Deidamia and Achilles are startled to notice someone has entered the garden. They do not know it is Lidoro and Libio.

DEIDAMIA: Someone's here.
Oh, what will become of me?
LIDORO: I hear voices over there. I see two figures.
LIBIO: Human-size, too.
LIDORO: We must know who they are.
LIBIO: Not so (fast)…
LIDORO: Well, what can I do?
LIBIO: Let's go back. Look how easy it is!
LIDORO: Idiot, what are you advising me to do?
How could I not know
who wanders this garden at night?
LIBIO: By not wanting to know.
DEIDAMIA: They're looking for us.
ACHILLES: Hide.
I will stay here to stop them from going further.
As long as they don't recognize you,
the rest doesn't matter.
DEIDAMIA: Woe is me! I leave my life in your hands.
(exits)
LIDORO: One of them turns his back.
LIBIO: So it seems.
LIDORO: And the other one holds his ground.
LIBIO: So it would seem.
LIDORO: Who's here?
ACHILLES: Who asks me?
LIDORO: A man who wants to know
how you entered this garden.

ACHILLES: Your doubt shows signs of impertinence.
You should ask yourself the same question.
I think you know how I came to this place.
LIDORO: I have reasons for my boldness.
ACHILLES: As do I.
LIDORO: And I must insist,
I must know who you are.
ACHILLES: And I insist on not telling you.
LIDORO: You force me to ask you.
ACHILLES: And I must respond in kind.

They both draw their swords, and are set to duel.

MUSICIANS (VO): Fugitive eyes
Over the garden wall.
Moisten their eyelashes
Upon the jasmines and carnations…
LIBIO: They have chosen the right time to sing! *(he is about to exit)*
LIDORO: What are you doing?
LIBIO: I am off to tell them to be quiet
Because two men shouldn't kill each other
to such a song!
LIDORO: Although you are valiant,
I'll know who you are.
ACHILLES: I am, such is valor's resolve,
The monster of this garden.
LIDORO: Name.
ACHILLES: No need of it.
LIDORO: Although you refuse to say it,
your death will tell me.

Ulysses enters the garden.

ULYSSES: What is this I hear?
Is it you who has left me sleepless night after night?
I must know you

Ulysses seizes Lidoro.

ACHILLES: (Well, this one comes mistaken, thank
God, and in my favor)

Achilles exits.

LIDORO: Gentleman, if you come seeking
As you have said, the monster of this garden
I will have you know
that you have just let him escape
And you have captured the one
who is also in search of him
ULYSSES: Do not defend yourself.
I do not foolishly seek your death,
But rather to make you Troy's conqueror.
I am Ulysses.
LIDORO: Ulysses?
Well, if that's your intent
Your diligence turns against you. I am Lidoro.
ULYSSES: You here, sir, in such dire straits!
LIDORO: From the outskirts of the garden,
while Deidamia's sadness was distracted by music,
I saw two figures:
one of them pretended to hide in the bushes.

I heard him call himself
"the monster of these gardens."
What else was I to do
knowing a man was hiding in the bushes
near my beloved?
This, my friend, is my sadness:
To think that Deidamia
knew someone was hiding there too
Because to think that
is to think that dark clouds stain the sun.
ULYSSES: To know who this man is
who makes us both restless
is to know the distance between Venus and Mars.
LIDORO: What man could hide day and night…
ULYSSES: I have reason to believe…
LIDORO: Great fear overcomes me…
ULYSSES: And not without cause….
LIDORO: And not in vain…
ULYSSES: With so many signs, I do believe…
LIDORO: If I doubt her disdain…
ULYSSES: Like the heavens have sent me…
LIDORO: Jealousy will claim me.

They leave the garden.

Scene Four

Dante, Lidoro, and King enter Deidamia's room.

KING: Daughter, I come with two pieces of news.
I have, on behalf of Acaya, Astrea's country…

where is she? Astrea?

Achilles appears dressed as Astrea.

ACHILLES: Right here.
KING: It gives me great anxiety to tell you that
Astrea's boat was wrecked at sea.
ACHILLES: Oh dear!
KING: And it makes sense to wonder how it can be
that one Astrea has perished, and another Astrea is
here with you.
ACHILLES: But sir…if I…when I arrived…?
LIDORO: Note her confusion.
KING: So much confusion causes deep doubt.
DEIDAMIA: It is foolish to give credit to that rumor.
There is no one who sets upon the sea
Who does not speak badly of hearsay;
it captivates him, or kills him.
KING: It very well could be hearsay
I leave it to time to disillusion us.
Meanwhile, let us leave this topic, and let us talk
Of something more important.
Lidoro, your father writes to me
Of how much he misses you;
And although Deidamia's health
Is not to be predicted from one day to the next
it is not possible to delay the wedding any longer.
And thus, I wish that
The wedding ceremony be held today.
Agree to this.

DEIDAMIA: You know I can only obey. I cannot choose my fate.

KING: With the torch they bring for you and Lidoro,
In demonstration of the love that burns
Between you, both of you shall be united.

ACHILLES: (When sorrows come, they come all at once, like an army!)

LIDORO: What should I do?

DANTE: Act like you don't care
Because from here to tomorrow
A thousand centuries may pass,
And a sad one can change her face in an instant.

MUSICIANS (VO):
To the nuptial bed of the pure wife
The crown of love is the highest trophy.
To the nuptial bed of the young lover
The crown of love is his sweetest employ
To the nuptial bed where love joins…

DEIDAMIA: Leave me all.

LIDORO: Leave?

DEIDAMIA: I must prepare myself for the ceremony.

LIDORO: Of course. Forgive me.

All leave quickly. Achilles slowly walks away.

DEIDAMIA: You leave me too, Astrea?

ACHILLES: Yes, ingrate,
Because your cruelty kills me
with such severity
That you've become a tyrant (to my eyes),
indeed of another time.

270

The lies must stop.
Because in time, we will all be disillusioned.
DEIDAMIA: I go without sleep, my love, I...
ACHILLES: Don't go on. Don't say a word.
DEIDAMIA: My life, my dear, listen...You are my sovereign.
ACHILLES: You're not getting married?
DEIDAMIA: Yes.
ACHILLES: But you love me?
DEIDAMIA: Obligation comes before passion
ACHILLES: A good excuse for a virtue born of blame.
DEIDAMIA: It is a but a forced, sad little effect;
here is its inclination, and there is respect.
Here it hates, and there it loves.
ACHILLES: Do me a good turn.
DEIDAMIA: What is that?
ACHILLES: Don't surrender to your sadness.

Sounds of war.

DEIDAMIA: What new beast is this?
Who has given such barbarous roar?
ACHILLES: This is the language of war
That calls forth great and terrible things,
That stirs the blood and enrages the heart
And with glorious disregard for life
Lets death stake her claim.

Sound of war increases.

Who can listen to such brave noise and not fight?

May the Greek empire live
And may Troy be destroyed in blood and fire!
Not one barbarous enemy will remain alive…
Forgive me, great power, that this portent
Has taken my attention to such an extreme.
ULYSSES: *[entering]* Achilles. Your death is near!
ACHILLES: What do you say?
Who are you talking to? I haven't understood.
ULYSSES: Excuse me, beautiful Astrea;
I am to speak you
Unawares, blind.
I thought – what delirium -
That I spoke with Achilles.
Such is he in my brain!
Forgive me.
Because now I see, woman,
That you are not Achilles
Nor could you ever be
Because the young man whom Mars,
God of the bloody duels,
Destines for glory,
The young one whom they give the last name
"Hero of the heavens
Honor of the gods,"
And who is said can use the stars as instruments
Of his divine influence,
The young man
whom the gods decree everlasting fame,
And whom history will set as an example,
Would never be caught
wearing such clothes as yours,

Would never take the time
to shave and use perfume
Because such foulness stains the soul
And doesn't beautify the body.
ACHILLES: Wait.
ULYSSES: You want me?
ACHILLES: You cannot assault someone's conscience
And leave him without words.
ULYSSES: What do you want?
ACHILLES: I only want …to have time to respond.
ULYSSES: How much time?
ACHILLES: A moment….
ULYSSES: I'll be back.
ACHILLES: Don't leave.
ULYSSES: Is it so urgent?
ACHILLES: Yes.
ULYSSES: What is it?
ACHILLES: I have resolved.
ULYSSES: Go on. Speak
ACHILLES: Prepare a horse for me,
And sound your instruments, Ulysses,
When they are ready.
I need to leave this palace.
ULYSSES: Whatever you wish, Astrea.

Ulysses leaves.

ACHILLES: It is done.
Fortune, you lost the day you lost Deidamia.
These adornments that
Effeminate my valor

I will give to Love's temple.
The disillusion is not your but mine
because what has been for me a beautiful garden
will be now in dispossession only an ancient trophy.
A snake renews its skin
And I (as a man) having left
the nuptial robes of Venus
will now only wear the martial robes of Mars.
Goodbye, sorry masquerade
Where my first love
Represented its most glorious effects.
Goodbye, flowers.
Goodbye, fountains.
Goodbye Deidamia.
DEIDAMIA: Where are you going
with sword in hand? Speak.
ACHILLES: I cannot say.
It is not possible to go on with our lie.
I know myself now.
DEIDAMIA: What? What are you saying?
ACHILLES: What is true. Ulysses called my name.
DEIDAMIA: You denied it.
ACHILLES: I couldn't.
DEIDAMIA: Your pride has caused this.
ACHILLES: Your betrayal had its effect!
DEIDAMIA: What?
ACHILLES: Goodbye, Deidamaia.
I don't want to see you in someone else's arms,
and thus must save my life.
The heavens keep me for Mars' tragedies,
Not for those of Venus

Goodbye again,
goodbye one and a thousand times.
DEIDAMIA: Hear me first
I, Achilles, lose my life if I lose you.
Don't leave me,
don't leave me to myself. I offer to be yours,
Even if fame, honor, and kingdom are at stake.
I am yours. Don't go.
ACHILLES: How can I leave you?
Lose life and honor, fame and glory.

Sounds of war.

Mars' voice calls to me.
And yet I choose not to respond to its spell.
DEIDAMIA: My love, sovereign.
MUSICIANS (VO): Love and war
Are glory and hell
Long live love
Let war be quelled.
ACHILLES: It is not a time of war but of love.
LIDORO: *[appears]* Who is in your arms, Deidamia?
ACHILLES: You'll know the monster of this garden.
DEIDAMIA: That's all I need!
LIDORO: Now I will see if another trick will free you
of me.
ACHILLES: I don't want lies to free me.
Rather I want valor and strength to do so.
MUSICIANS (VO): Love and war
Are glory and hell
Long live love.

Let war be quelled.
DEIDAMIA: Now that all in life is lost, may the least
of things be lost too. Father!
KING: *[appears]* What's this? Astrea, you fight with
Lidoro?
ACHILLES: That lie is over.
I am ashamed to hear such a name.
I am Achilles.
I have been a traitor to your house
Because I was in love with Deidamia
And now she is my wife.
So, do what you will.
KING: Kill him.
DEIDAMIA: Woe is me.
ULYSSES: *[appears]* I am taking him with me.

Thetis appears.

THETIS: Listen all of you to Thetis.
Today is the fatal day
That threatened Achilles with auguries;
The trance
in which he finds himself is clear sign of this.
It is from this that I wished to free him,
thinking I could spare him from the call of war,
but instead it has been peace
that has brought him and us to this very juncture.
Don't take away, valiant Greeks
your happiness by killing that
for which you live in wait for.
It is not a time of war but of love.

KING: I will forget my worries.

LIDORO: And I will desist in my jealousy.

LIBIO: *[appears]* Long live Achilles.

KING: Give Deidamia your hand

DEIDAMIA: I am happy.

ACHILLES: Great fortune is mine.

DANTE: *[appears]* And so as a prodigious witness I say, thus ends the monster in the garden.

END OF PLAY

Caridad Svich

Bio:

Caridad Svich is a US Latina playwright, translator, lyricist and editor. She received a 2012 OBIE Award for Lifetime Achievement in the theatre, and the 2011 American Theatre Critics Association Primus Prize for her play *The House of the Spirits*, based on the novel by Isabel Allende. She has been short-listed for the PEN Award in Drama four times, including in the year 2012 for her play *Magnificent Waste*. Among her key works: *12 Ophelias, Alchemy of Desire/Dead-Man's Blues, Any Place But Here, Iphigenia...a rave fable, Fugitive Pieces, GUAPA, The Way of Water, The Tropic of X*, and *Love in the Time of Cholera*, based on the novel by Garcia Marquez. She has edited several books on theatre including *Out of Silence: Censorship in Theatre & Performance* (Eyecorner Press), *Trans-Global Readings* and *Theatre in Crisis?* (both for Manchester University Press) and *Divine Fire* (BackStage Books). She has translated nearly all of Federico Garcia Lorca's plays and also dramatic works by Julio Cortazar, Antonio Buero Vallejo and contemporary plays from Mexico, Cuba and Catalonia. She is alumna playwright of New Dramatists, founder of NoPassport theatre alliance & press (http://www.nopassport.org), Drama Editor of *Asymptote* journal of literary translation, associate editor of Routledge/UK's *Contemporary Theatre Review* and contributing editor of *TheatreForum*. She holds an MFA in Theatre-Playwriting from UCSD, and has taught creative writing and playwriting at Bard College, Barnard College, Bennington College, Ohio State University, Rutgers University-New Brunswick, and Yale School of Drama. She is an entry in the *Oxford Encyclopedia of Latino Literature*. Website: www.caridadsvich.com

Printed in Great Britain
by Amazon

84258335R00162